Oct 2019

CROSSHAIRS

MATT FITZPATRICK

Frank,

Thank you!

Enjoy.

Matt

A JUSTIN MCGEE

MYSTERY

CROSSHAIRS

MATT FITZPATRICK

GREEN PLACE BOOKS | *Brattleboro, Vermont*

Printed in the United States

10 9 8 7 6 5 4 3 2 1

GREEN WRITERS PRESS is a Vermont-based publisher whose mission is to spread a message of hope and renewal through the words and images we publish. Throughout we will adhere to our commitment to preserving and protecting the natural resources of the earth. To that end, a percentage of our proceeds will be donated to environmental activist groups and the author's focus on preserving the Cape Cod seashore. Green Writers Press gratefully acknowledges support from individual donors, friends, and readers to help support the environment and our publishing initiative. GREEN PLACE BOOKS curates books that tell literary and compelling stories with a focus on writing about place.

GREEN
PLACE
BOOKS

Giving Voice to Writers & Artists Who Will Make the World a Better Place

Green Writers Press | Brattleboro, Vermont
www.greenwriterspress.com

ISBN: 978-1-7320815-8-1

COVER DESIGN: Asha Hossain
BOOK DESIGN: Hannah Wood

For information, please contact the author at mfitz71@comcast.net

PRINTED ON PAPER WITH PULP THAT COMES FROM FSC-CERTIFIED FORESTS, MANAGED FOR-
ESTS THAT GUARANTEE RESPONSIBLE ENVIRONMENTAL, SOCIAL, AND ECONOMIC PRACTICES BY
LIGHTNING SOURCE. ALL WOOD PRODUCT COMPONENTS USED IN BLACK AND WHITE, STANDARD
COLOR OR SELECT COLOR PAPERBACK BOOKS, UTILIZING EITHER CREAM OR WHITE BOOKBLOCK
PAPER,, THAT ARE MANUFACTURED IN THE LAVERGNE, TENNESSEE PRODUCTION CENTER ARE
SUSTAINABLE FORESTRY INITIATIVE (SFI) CERTIFIED SOURCING.

The characters in this novel are all indeed based on real people in my life.

Many of the events are also based on factual experiences.

The names of course have been changed to protect both the innocent and the guilty.

Some of the characters will be immediately recognizable, while others will leave the reader guessing.

And I won't fold under questioning . . .

Enjoy!

— Boston's North Shore, Winter 2018

"His heart is soft. Time will harden it."

— Mario Puzo

"Maybe there is a beast. Maybe it's us?"

— William Golding

All for Kailee and Nicole . . .

CROSSHAIRS

MATT FITZPATRICK

Chapter 1

Jus and Meyer

"Okay old friend," said *Justin McGee* as he ordered his second Harpoon Ale at the North End's landmark Sail Loft bar. "Hope you are up for this. Time to break your cherry."

Meyer listened intently while sipping on a lime-infused Perrier.

"There's a piece of freelance contract work hanging out there on the street that Darby gave me the heads-up on," Jus continued. "A 'cold case,' if you will. It's so long outstanding that nobody has exclusive rights to the job, but Darb guarantees that whoever finally raises this barn will be paid in full by some boys from Hartford. Seems that with all of the chaos in our business over the past couple of years, nobody can organize a proper hit."

Meyer chuckled. "You freaks in your business actually act like this is a world with regulations and proper etiquette. What a joke!"

Jus gave a quick smile, and then explained that this was not a dress rehearsal, and if he wanted in, he needed to quickly adopt the "go hard or go home" attitude.

Meyer nodded.

"Anyway," Jus went on, "we have a female, age thirty-two . . ."

"What!" Meyer interjected. "We're gonna ice a chick!?"

"Meyer. This isn't the playground sandbox, and this is no Girl Scout selling s'mores and thin mints!" Jus leaned forward and continued in a low voice. "Her name is Crasha Moloney. She grew up in the Southie projects, the only daughter of hardworking, second-generation Irish. She definitely ran hardscrabble during her youth, but she kicked it up a notch when she started running with some of the neighborhood players. She took care of them the old-fashioned way in the backs of IROC-Zs, and they gratefully reciprocated by bringing her 'brown' bag lunches—you follow?"

Meyer responded with a small chuckle.

Jus continued. "So this Crasha got a little out of line a couple of years ago when the gang put the snips on some Ivy League, wide-eyed frat boy who was home for the summer and who hung out at Suffolk Downs trying to be cool 'cause he had seen *Goodfellas* one too many times. He'd throw Daddy's money around, which of course immediately garnered the attention of Crasha's crew. She played nice-nice with him one night as they bet on the races and he bought her gimlets. They arranged a second date for the following week, and he assured her that he would bring plenty of bills so that they could bet big and celebrate in a commensurate fashion. As they parted goodbye, she thanked him with an old-school, parking-lot 'smoothie,' after which they eagerly set up their next encounter.

"The next week, Frat Boy and Crasha made quite a time of it, while of course Crasha's Southie crew looked on with saliva-soaked chins. When the night ended, Frat Boy had indeed proven his mettle and ended up walking away with profits, plus his original stash, which all totaled about forty thousand. Crasha lured Frat Boy to her car for the customary goodbye hummer, when all of a sudden Venus, one of the crew, removed the back of Frat's skull with the business end of a crow bar. Frat's clam-chowder-consistency brain matter and what remained of his future began to soil the racetrack parking lot, as Crasha's crew politely relieved him of the burden of his currency. This was not her intention, as she did not want him killed, but in the end, for half of the take, she could live with whatever feeble amount of guilt his demise might conjure up.

"Frat's father was devastated, and unfortunately for Crasha he was quite well connected with the good 'community-minded' folks at Suffolk Downs, who provided him with plenty of video footage of Crasha setting up her mark in the stands at the racetrack on those warm summer nights. Frat's dad put the contract out on the street, but there was a lack of follow up due to his having a stroke and ending up at Sunny Acres gnawing on a jigsaw puzzle. He always liked the corner pieces best."

Jus paused, took a sip of his beer, and asked, "What's your take, Meyer? You in?"

"Yeah, man," said Meyer eagerly. "Let's take this slut out and make a score. But with Frat's old man all messed up, how do we know we'll get paid?"

Jus replied, "Darby told me that the fee is in escrow with some two-bit weasel corpse-kicking lawyer from Everett. Fifty thousand cash. Darb is trustworthy—he's one of a dying breed of old-school players who still believe in honor and all of the other tenets of that farce of a code." Justin sighed. "Something to be said for honor, Meyer."

"Yeah. Something to be said . . ."

Justin then shot Meyer a penetrating look and asked, "So how are you feeling, old friend?"

Meyer leaned back and grinned. "Like it's the first day of the rest of my life . . ."

A Few Days Later

The hit was set for the following Thursday night. Jus learned from Darby that Crasha was scheduled to be on a charter-boat cruise in Boston Harbor aboard the *Annabelle Lee*, a sturdy forty-two-foot cabin cruiser owned and operated by Captain Henry Panke. However, the pilot duties were being subbed out to Captain Caleb Frost, a Gloucesterman who was always looking for extra charter work.

Jus and Meyer had borrowed a mutual friend's twenty-five-foot Sea Ray that was kept at Waterboat Marina, next to the Marriott Long Wharf. This was the perfect vessel for the job—she was sturdy and fast, but not flashy enough as to attract attention. The spacious cabin had ample space for hiding weapons and ancillary equipment.

Jus and Meyer watched across the small channel as Crasha boarded the boat that, for tonight, was chartered by an organization called Boston Women in Business, whose members began arriving either by BMW 7 Series or merely traveling the short distance on foot from Boston's illustrious Financial District. All sported stunningly colored attire or tight business suits that radiated their financial success. As they gingerly boarded the vessel one by one, the sheer level of physical attractiveness would have made a Victoria's Secret photographer envious.

When Crasha arrived, she stealthily extended her hand to a handsome man in a captain's uniform, who helped her aboard. He had the hard features of someone whose skin often was met with stinging salt spray, and yet he possessed boyish, innocent good looks that Crasha immediately wished to exploit and corrupt. For her, opportunities to score grew like dandelions flourishing in a field of cowshit.

"I'm Crasha. You must be the handsome captain, just like in all of the romance novels?" If she were from Georgia, she might have punctuated her comment with "I do declare . . ."

"Yes, ma'am," answered the man in uniform. "I'm Captain Caleb Frost and I'll be hosting you this evening, along with my first mate, Sputnik. We're from Gloucester but we're in Boston tonight filling in for a friend to make sure that you and your colleagues have an enjoyable evening."

"I'll hold you to that, Captain," laughed Crasha.

Captain Caleb was not particularly fond of outings of this sort, but work was work, and it was a light task indeed. No-wake speed around the harbor, keep the music low and the ice cold, and above all just maintain the smiles on the guests' faces. The Italian designer handbags unmistakably assured him of some decent cash tips from all those leaving the vessel with a shoulder-weight buzz.

Captain Frost had gotten the gig through a one-off referral phone call from Henry Panke to Captain Tommy, who was chartering in Florida at the time, which had gone as follows:

"Hey, Tommy. Reason for my call is that I need a freelancer for a gig on Thursday night. Someone, ya know, reliable, 'cause it's one of these fancy-ass corporate gigs out of the Vulture District down the street. All high-powered skirts with Louis Vuitton shoes and Birkin bags. I need someone who has the skill, the brains, and the looks. Someone who won't take these broads out into international waters and start slapping asses. You know anyone who can handle the responsibility? Someone who is . . . feebly mature? You know anyone?"

Tommy's immediate response was a resounding, "No. Nobody with a crank, anyway . . ."

They both laughed.

After a moment's thought, Tommy said, "Actually, yeah, Henry. There's a guy I know out of Gloucester who's a straight shooter. Always looking for work. Reliable, and in fact he's been a bit down on his luck recently. I wouldn't at all mind seeing you give him the gig. You won't be disappointed. I'll e-mail you his info."

Henry responded, "Sounds great, Tommy. I appreciate it. Hey, if you're up to it, I'll trade you my prude, yuppie, Boston banker–type group for one of your Sunshine State titty-party outings."

"*Any*time, Henry. Anytime. I need a nice calm wine-and-cheese group of passengers to get things back to normal in this sideshow of a state. They oughta just throw a tent over the whole swamp from Jacksonville to the Keys and call it the Not-So-Traveling Circus. No wonder the whole damn state is shaped like an alligator's cock . . ."

"Tommy," Henry interjected. "What's the matter? What's going on?"

Captain Tommy replied, "I'm just pissed, that's all. Really upset. Heading to Key West with four couples who initially positioned themselves as a bunch of Upper East Side yuppies who were lifelong friends looking for a cruise trip in order to celebrate one of their fortieth birthdays. Turns out they met yesterday at the airport for the first time after corresponding over the smut-net and they're using my vessel as a swingers' tropical paradise. I'm too old for this shit!"

Henry rolled his eyes, whispering to himself, "And this guy is complaining . . ."

Tommy continued. "Yeah, Henry, these people won't friggin' listen. They refuse to listen to their captain! I told them, 'Fine. Fine. You can have all the damn sex you want, but keep it below deck! I can't have the damn Coast Guard come by and see us presenting a starboard-side version of Sodom and Gomorrah!"

Henry just shook his head. "Wow, Tommy. Seems like a tough charter. You gonna make it?"

"I'll live . . ."

"Well, Tommy, my friend. I wish you well with trying to get them properly clad."

To Henry, it was clear that the salt air had rotted out Tommy's brain.

Jus and Meyer on Surveillance

Hawk-like, Jus and Meyer watched as the group gathered on the aft deck of the *Annabelle Lee* and proceeded to exchange greetings, pour wine, and pass around shrimp cocktails.

Meyer broke the silence. "Okay, Jus. This is your outing. What's my role here? Can I hop onto that boat, have my way with the mermaids, kill that Crasha bitch, and be on my way after hoisting the Jolly Roger?"

"No offense, old friend, but just steer the damn boat, and keep your mind on wind and tide. I'm only going to get one shot at her, and I want a clean hit with zero collateral damage. The good thing is that she is a smoker in all senses of the word."

Meyer smiled, nodding.

Jus continued, "So at some point she'll be out on deck for either a cigarette or a 'who-knows-what' type of break. Maybe we can get her out there with minimal others present."

Meyer interjected, "Hey, Jus. So we off this broad—then what? How do we get outta here without the damn Coast Guard or somebody firing some kinda torpedo shit at us?"

Jus shook his head, smiling. "The beauty of a water hit," he explained, "is that there isn't a Coast Guard boat on every corner, and the airport is only a mile away. Darb set it up so that after the hit, we throw the hammer down on this tub and burn over to the airport dock, where Darb is having us whisked off by a van that will slam us up Route One before the Coast Guard even gets to the *Annabelle Lee*. We pull the drain plug once we're at the airport, and she'll sink. Fast. Our mutual friend will end up wondering what became of his treasured vessel, but fuck it—sea travel is hazardous . . ."

Meyer nodded, looking around at the soon-to-be-sunken boat.

Jus continued, "She does not have to be reported as stolen, 'cause no one expects the owner to check on the boat more than once a week or so. They'll certainly find the boat, but it will be a couple of days and we'll be long gone. Hence, the reason that you have gloves on and I figured that you would not need new slippers. . ." He glanced up at the sky, then added, "We just need to wait until it's dark."

A few minutes later, Captain Caleb and Sputnik threw the lines and the *Annabelle Lee* blew her horn twice and entered the slightly chopped waters of Boston Harbor.

Even before the boat was fully underway, the charter guests appeared to be having a wonderful time on the aft deck, busily networking, sipping wine, and even singing along, a few of them, to the insipid Celine Dion mix that Caleb was instructed to play on the boat's salt-infused sound system.

The sun was setting fast as Caleb slowly putt-putted at the usual charter-boat speed out into the harbor toward the southern side, passing by the New England Aquarium to starboard. As the day gave way to a warm, late-summer Boston evening, Caleb noticed that the wind had begun to subside. A steadying calm settled upon the vessel.

Caleb turned to Sputnik with a puzzled look and said, "Hey, I don't hear the guests, just music. That's weird. Why don't you head on back and make sure that they all didn't just fall into the drink? Yeah, that would be a lot of fun, trying to fish them all out of the harbor at 2:00 A.M. . . ."

Sputnik returned a couple of minutes later with a mile-wide grin and a deep chuckle, and Caleb knew this meant that there was nothing funny except that his warped-minded first mate Sputnik was residing in some type of unexpected and premature slice of heaven.

"Hey, Skip. You won't believe this. Our cargo of panty-wearing CEOs have reconvened in the salon below deck."

"Yeah?" replied Captain Frost. "Whadda they doing? Pulling out a fishing scale to weigh all the gold they're sporting? Or maybe holding a golf clinic?"

"Not exactly" replied the first mate. "How's the electric system on this vessel? Do we have extra power to feed a few more outlets?"

"Shit," replied Caleb. "C'mon. . . Really?"

The first mate just kept grinning.

Finally Caleb asked, "C'mon, Sput'. You're killin' me. . . ."

Sputnik's dopey grin, along with his lack of verbal response, confirmed Caleb's immediate suspicion. He'd seen this before. He always wondered why shit like this always had to happen at sea?

"Your wheel, Sput'," said Caleb as he nudged his first mate toward the helm and proceeded to walk softly toward the aft deck so that he could look into the salon.

There, Caleb saw every Coast Guard cadet's fantasy come to life. Down below in the salon, the Boston Women in Business Association was revealed as a clandestine lesbian swinger group and they were in the process of reinventing the pretzel.

There was more lube sloshing around than there was water in the harbor.

Man, thought Caleb. *I'm getting too old for this. . . . Maybe my Puritan ancestry is still suppressing me. . . .*

For Crasha, meanwhile, that second wine had begun to wrap its soft leather belt around her seemingly forever-moving waist when she noticed Matilda Chong.

Chong was one of the most respected senior international bond analysts at one of Boston's must illustrious boutique wealth-management firms. Matilda had spent her early childhood in Beijing. Around the time of her fifth birthday, her father disappeared in the massive city's central market square, where he sold chickens from a rickety gray wooden barrow in the fond hope of being able to bring home a modest fish and a crust of bread for his struggling family. A few days later, Matilda's mom received word that, on the day of his disappearance, her husband had looked confused before falling face-first into an ankle-deep puddle of muddy water.

The word around the city square was that Matilda's dad had died of either acute emphysema (self-induced or not) or good old-fashioned syphilis. Nobody really cared one way or the other, but because of Chinese traditions that have been maintained in the marketplace for thousands of years, wagers were indeed taken among his peers.

Matilda's mom swore that her daughter would never have to grow up in that hell. Fortunately, she had a contact in Boston's Chinatown district, so she immediately ran and grabbed their erstwhile emergency fund, which of course would otherwise be stolen by sundown by her late husband's supposed best "friends," and headed for the airport.

As soon as Matilda and her mother were settled in Boston, where Matilda impressed her grade-school teachers by learning English quickly and excelling in mathematics. Before long, in fact, she began to blow her teachers' minds with her seemingly extraterrestrial ability to analyze patterns within the financial markets.

By the time she graduated from high school, Matilda was offered full scholarships by several of the city's finest institutions of higher education, and she selected a full four-year scholarship to Boston College's Carroll School of Management. Her attitude was: "Screw those snobs at Harvard and MIT — they're on the wrong side of the river." Matilda had her sights on living near Fenway Park and taking the Green Line to class

At some point during her exemplary college career, Matilda learned another life lesson, one that her mother would never have dared to teach her. As much as Matilda loved the prospect of making money, and as much as she loved baseball, more than anything else she loved the perfect form of a woman. She was proud of her formidable analytical skills, but she was prouder still of her ability to truly appreciate the beauty of God's greatest gift to the world.

Her first time came during office hours at BC with a female teaching assistant from Wales. They were discussing some market anomaly when Matilda said to herself, *No, I will not die in a ditch in some muddy sewer*, and she proceeded to share with her mentor the wettest kiss ever shared between two human beings. The proverbial "desk-clearing" occurred within sixty seconds. Matilda had never tasted a sweeter wine.

Matilda had succeeded in making it in America's home town, but as the ever-so-successful Chinese executive crossed the salon aboard the *Annabelle Lee*, what shocked Crasha most and set her tingling was the unparalleled power of Matilda's soft skin, which radiated a confidence and perfection that seemed to have come from a silent field of sweet-scented lemon grass.

Matilda quickly noticed Crasha's hungry stare. Their mutual attraction was unstoppable, and the voluptuous Asian instantly felt a primal heat coursing over every inch of her body.

Matilda slowly extricated from her Birkin bag the most impressive and convincing "toy" that Crasha had ever seen. Crasha yearned for it to touch her. To know her. To "convince" her on every level. As Crasha continued to survey the tool, her mouth began to water.

Not that she was a nymphomaniac, but, in the bedroom, sex gave Crasha power. It made her feel needed. In the most natural way, sex gave her a badly needed identity.

In a low, insinuating voice, Matilda said, "I have something for you. A gift of sorts, and I do not give many. However, in this case I feel that it is well deserved."

As Matilda slowly entered her, Crasha sighed loudly, and the sound of the party ceased and the oceans stopped the ebb and flow of the ancient tide.

Meanwhile, Justin and Meyer were about a hundred yards from the stern of the *Annabelle Lee*—just enough distance to maintain surveillance without drawing attention unnecessarily.

Meyer's binoculars were stuck to his face like crazy glue as he gazed upon the scene openly visible through the stern window.

Jus and Meyer noticed that the *Annabel Lee*'s deck was extremely quiet, when all of a sudden a bolt of lightning struck.

Crasha was a little startled at first, but she certainly wanted to fit in with the crowd.

At her first taste of the sweetness, it was the dream of dreams. She rolled over and folded for her friend for the night until the sweat commanded her perfect completion.

Crasha needed a cigarette break and walked, or rather limped, onto the aft deck of the vessel. The two assassins figured from the unsteady way she moved that perhaps she was tipsy on wine, or maybe a bit seasick.

Crasha stood by the stern rail and fired up a Capri. It was amazing that, although she was so rough around the edges, she could still fit in with this upper-crust crowd, but Crasha was quite the chameleon and could change her look and demeanor, much like Clark Kent in a phone booth. She took a drag, blew it out and stared up at the stars.

This was a one-in-a-million perfect chance for Justin. He quickly went below deck and grabbed the long-range rifle. He checked the barrel and scope, saying to Meyer, "Bring us a little closer without attracting attention, and then maintain a quiet five-knot, no-wake speed. It's relatively calm, so there should be minimal wave bumps."

Justin carefully prepared his Remington 700 long-barrel sniper rifle. It was a beast that shot .300 Winchester Magnum rounds and was accurate from a thousand yards away. While it technically was not military grade, it had insane stopping power. It was the number-one bolt-action rifle of all time. The strength of the three steel rings of its receiver, paired with its hammer-forged barrel, made it a formidable tool of Justin's trade.

Ostensibly, the weapon was made for big-game hunting, but he had other, more-lucrative, uses for it. Jus viewed his occupation as a true art form. He was a surgeon behind that trigger, and—unfortunately for his targets—his accuracy was uncanny.

Meanwhile, Meyer dutifully complied and the engines grew quiet.

Jus set the rifle on the boat's bow pulpit, where, in the darkness of this pleasant evening, he could remain unnoticed. Without feeling or emotion, his mind slowed, as did his heart rate. He felt the strange calm known only to starfish.

Then: *Pssst . . .*

No, not the sound of a whisper. It was the sound of the sniper's bullet leaving Justin's rifle before quickly entering the temple of Crasha's skull.

Strangely, she also remained quite calm, as though—if only for a millisecond—she had an acceptance and even a strange understanding of what just transpired.

The slug entered and exited her brain and then lodged itself in the fiberglass of the *Annabelle Lee* with very little sound, certainly nothing that could be heard above the din of the twin diesel engines.

She slumped over a deck chair in an unnaturally contorted position that exuded a strange kind of peace. The spattered blood painted a strip of modern art on the fiberglass wall behind her, and quickly began to pool on the spotless white aft deck.

Justin ran back to the helm station of the Sea Ray and firmly grabbed a side rail. "Give it hell, Meyer!" he hissed. "Get to the fuckin' airport dock, now!"

Meyer threw down both throttles and cut their course hard to port. The boat made a beeline toward their awaiting getaway vehicle.

Once at the dock, they gathered their bags and headed up the gangway, but only after Justin had plunged his arm into the no-longer "dirty water" of the bilge and pulled open the boat's drain plug. The six bullets that Justin had fired through the hull below the Sea Ray's waterline would certainly help quicken the sinking process as the vessel eagerly awaited a night's rest on the silty floor of historic Boston Harbor in her sepulcher by the sea. . . .

Meanwhile, back aboard the *Annabelle Lee*, outright chaos had ensued upon the discovery of Crasha's lifeless body. The group erupted in sheer panic, but Captain Caleb merely shook his head and said to Sputnik, "So, not only did we have our passengers engaging in an orgy tonight, but now they're getting friggin' shot! This is not good for business. What the hell happened?!"

The women on board screamed and demanded to be brought back to shore at once. In their state of terror, the club roamed the deck aimlessly, like a casting call for *The Walking Dead*.

Caleb tried to see if he could get any vitals from Crasha's body, but to no avail—she was dead.

What the group, as well as the captain and crew, did not know was that they had just encountered the work of Boston's most deadly assassin. And it was work flawlessly executed. If Justin were a painter, he would have his own wing at the Museum of Fine Arts.

The Next Day

"I really don't friggin' need this," Detective Warnock muttered to himself as the dock workers managed to secure the cables to the hull of Justin and Meyer's getaway boat.

The veteran detective only thought of two things on this fair-weather Sunday: Where am I going to watch the Pats' preseason game? and how soon can I collect my pension?

Warnock closely watched with feigned interest as the battered vessel was hoisted out of the water by the marine transport crane and slowly lowered onto the concrete next to the dock.

As the boat kissed the cement, Warnock noticed all of the bullet holes that had enabled the quick sinking. He thought to himself, Poor bastard that owns this boat. The thing has more holes in it than Montreal's St. Catherine Street . . .

Suddenly Warnock was approached by an impeccably dressed man who looked to be around fifty. Obviously a G-man, thought Warnock.

"I'm Special Agent Caras, FBI Boston Office," the man said. "What do we have here, detective?"

Warnock responded, "Really? They feel the need to send in the spooks to stare at a shitty Swiss-cheese-hulled boat? Shouldn't you guys still be in the confessional box after what happened with Whitey and Stevie?"

Special Agent Caras was not amused.

"We were instructed to visit the scene of a crime. A gruesome assassination, actually. We would appreciate any and all cooperation that you might provide."

Warnock gave him a short gesture of the hand, as if to say, "Whatever. In the end, I really don't give a shit."

He then turned to face Special Agent Caras and said, "Bottom line. We have what appears to have been two perps who committed the murder while on the water, and this was their means of getaway. They scuttled the boat in order to literally wash away any evidence. At this time, we have no way to identify the shooter. You can hang out all you want. Hope you brought a picnic lunch and a few beers, 'cause it's gonna be a long afternoon. Hey, with all of that fancy FBI gear you've got in your van, do you think that you can conjure up some portable TV so we can at least watch the Pats game?"

Chapter 2

Meyer
(One Month Earlier)

Panting. Muscles pulsating as they drown in acid. Lungs relentlessly burning . . .

Meyer had completed six Boston Marathons and was insanely immersed in training for number seven. His thoughts briefly flashed on the tragic Marathon bombing:

Fuck those Eastern European cowardly radical Islamic terrorists—bunch of godless sons of bitches . . .

At least they enjoyed our country while they were alive and free . . .

Welfare, food stamps, free health care . . .

So said Yackoff Smirnoff: "What a country."

Meyer reflected that the only redemption was that one terrorist was dead and then nicknamed "Speed Bump"—evidently run over by his "loyal" brother. Said loyal brother was in federal custody and was certainly enjoying prison life by dressing up as Little Bo Peep and becoming quite "popular" with his fellow inmates. Meyer prayed that the Aryan Nation crew would conveniently forget the K-Y . . .

As Meyer's lungs pleaded a Roberto Duran cry for *"no más,"* he searched for air that would not be so easily delivered.

Meyer's life was at least consistent—decent-enough career during the day, and his nights engulfed in ceaseless training.

The Boston Marathon is where legends are made, as Meyer learned as a wide-eyed kid standing with his dad on the Commonwealth Avenue sidelines and watching Boston's version of the Running of the Bulls.

Unlike the majority of his friends, Meyer neither drank nor smoked. Instead, he taunted his mirror every morning while reminding himself that he *will* be the best, owing to his Adonis-like body and Apollo-like clarity of mind.

As Meyer rounded his final lap at record speed, he called it a day. He wanted to preserve every bit of energy for tomorrow's military-style workout.

Afterwards, heading slowly toward his van, he suddenly experienced a profound adrenaline rush, accompanied by an epiphany that, despite so many unforeseen obstacles, he was indeed blessed.

Blessed by whom, he was still uncertain.

Once again, clutching his watch-timer like Charlton Heston clutched his rifle, he could boast to himself a record training time. He tapped his clicker, painstakingly extricated himself from his wheelchair, and slid into the driver's seat with the amazing strength of his powerful arms. He reached down, gathered up the custom-made racing chariot, and folded it into place beside him, where it would ride shotgun.

Meyer was proud that he had served his county with valor, even though he then returned from a sandy hellhole with no use of his legs, due to a particularly feisty roadside bomb. Yet he would not be deterred in seeking excellence. He was grateful to have made it home, and to have placed in the top ten in the Marathon's wheelchair division for six years running.

While at times he was envious of his college classmates with their Porsches, piece-of-ass wives, and McMansions in Wellesley, he had to remind himself that they had spent their junior years abroad in London.

Meyer spent his in Fallujah . . .

As Meyer sped away, he thought that he would check up on Justin, his best friend and college roommate. Since Jus was an only child, Meyer served not only as a best friend but also as a surrogate brother. When Meyer was in the hospital in Germany, being treated for his horrific battle wounds, it was Jus who dropped everything and flew over to Deutschland in order to spend several days by his bedside.

Yeah, Meyer certainly could have bit the bag of self-pity with an attitude griping, "Shit. I'm a black, underemployed cripple . . ." But that sentiment was reserved for those who embraced weakness. In no way was Meyer anyone's victim.

Jus was the kindest soul—the most selfless soul he had ever met—and yet it was Meyer and only Meyer who was aware of Justin's darker side, with a soul that waltzed with shadows . . .

Justin (One Month Earlier)

Steam . . .

The shower head continued to explode, intermittently unveiling an Aphrodite-like vision—warm and exposed by an unrelenting, shameless cascade. Justin McGee was no stranger to the mirror himself, and his gritty, hard Boston looks graced him with many opportunities for female law-firm staffers to drive up his water bill during extended lunch meetings.

Jus watched as his partner for the afternoon warmed her body and vigorously attempted to wash away the hour's events. He remembered the moments of soft sheets. Turning over the pillow in order to find the only available coolness, while busy hands feverishly accepted warm invitations.

Jus's mind wandered back to when, earlier in the afternoon, his intern giggled as they boarded the elevator. While said livery should have gone down to the depths of his own personal hell, he gently pressed the button for the fifth floor as he ran his other hand through her soft, gently curled, sepia-colored hair.

When they crossed the threshold of his condo entrance, Jus offered her a drink. She politely declined because she was technically "on the clock," but it did not take him long to convince her that she needed just a little confidence booster in order to ensure a pleasant afternoon.

He kissed her slowly. Jus loved deep kisses. This was one of the feeble lifelines that connected him with some semblance of humanity. He was firmly convinced that a deep kiss was the only redeeming, life-giving act that might save the doomed soul of someone who spent so much time destroying life.

He slowly unbuttoned her silk blouse and found the rear zipper on her plaid skirt, revealing a glowing purple ensemble from Frederick's of Hollywood.

She quietly began to giggle. The afternoon liquor was already seeping past her stomach, which had been empty since lunch the day before, lest she gain six ounces.

He ran his finger up and down her washboard-tight stomach, and her breathing became feverish.

She immediately grabbed Jus's belt and then touched right below, indicating with a little giggle that she was quite satisfied with his natural endowment.

She knelt down and discovered him.

After a few minutes, Jus gently guided her upward, cradled her body in his arms, and carried her to his bed, as he had done dozens of times before with so many who naively thought that it was his first such encounter, as even with his slowly advancing age, he could still play shy-boy while surveilling the open field of office cubicles.

He laid her down and quietly slid inside.

Their rhythm and syncopation was as perfect as if it had been composed by Gene Krupa.

Her panting quickened dramatically, and he was surprised by the quickness and intensity of her climax as she dug her newly painted nails into his well-defined back.

He made it clear that he was not quite finished, but after her loudly vocalized satisfaction, Jus did not take long at all . . .

They lay quietly in each other's arms for a few minutes before Justin asked his intern to speak to him. To tell him how she was feeling. Justin understood his own narcissism, but he had a detached, almost scientific curiosity about people who had actual feelings. He had no idea what brought him more emptiness: the simplicity of "knowing" his office assistant in the biblical sense, or the fact that he was due at a deposition in forty-five minutes

Both promised a similar level of boredom.

If they only knew . . .

He had wowed his peers at Boston College Law School—top 10 percent of his class, yet he could down three shots of Jaeger at Mary Ann's as fast as the tide would rip out of the Chatham cut. "Typical sauced-up Irish," his old girlfriend's Greek father would say.

Jus always managed to get by with a stiff middle finger in the air, and a jawbone set with equal conviction.

His Great-Uncle Rick introduced him to the Rod & Gun club when he was still just a tadpole swimming toward nine years old. It was all very simple. Set up the target and aim the weapon. Very easy. And the utter simplicity and finality of the act of firing a gun both confused Jus and sparked his interest. The other club members would tease Uncle Rick about his nephew's uncanny accuracy, as well as his seemingly pure sense of "solace" behind the trigger.

Justin remembered how, as a young kid, he had loved staying over at Uncle Rick's house from time to time, for there was always some kind of indefinable action and buzz about the place. He never understood how Rick had so many friends, or why they would constantly stop by unannounced, or the strange hours when they would call on his aging uncle.

Rick and his friends always seemed to gather at the dining room table in a Sunday-afternoon, NFL-huddle formation. They constantly chain-smoked and sipped whiskey, and Jus remembered being able to see only the bottom five feet of the room beneath the ten-foot ceiling, for the upper half was a veritable Benson & Hedges–induced fog bank.

Uncle Rick never married, and there were always whispers and rumors about Uncle Rick that Jus noticed when he attended wakes and holiday cookouts. It was almost as though certain members of the family were in some way frightened by him. This made no sense to young Jus, for Rick treated his nephew like a courtly prince, and there was always had plenty of room for him in Rick's spacious, four-bedroom home—not an ostentatious dwelling by any means, but certainly rather excessive for a confirmed bachelor with a relatively modest lifestyle.

That particular night proved most interesting. Right around midnight, roughly a dozen of Rick's friends gathered at the house, all of them arriving within twenty minutes of one another.

Young Jus could not really understand the conversation, other than that most of the words began with a very pronounced "f," but it seemed to revolve around someone being hurt during a basketball game that involved the son of Uncle Rick's friend Lisa.

Jus was always curious about Lisa, for she would only visit Rick very late in the middle of the night. They would go into Rick's bedroom and shut the door. Jus thought it curious that Lisa seemed to enjoy a certain muffled type of singing that would go on for around an hour, and then Rick would walk her to her car.

Anyway, all that Jus could gather from the heated conversation downstairs was that Lisa's son had volunteered at the community center as a basketball coach, and that a fight broke out over a two-bit pickup game, which resulted in two forwards for the opposing team being sent to the emergency room and Lisa's son being thrown on ice in the hospital basement after encountering the business end of an eight-inch hunting knife.

Uncle Rick slammed his fist on the table and growled, "I want that motherless son of a bitch dead! I don't give a flying fuck if he's sixteen! *Leo!* Who do we have who can get to this prick while he's still in the hospital, so that when he leaves Intensive Care, it's only to be rolled down to the fuckin' morgue while he waits for the hearse?"

Leo replied, "Rick, I got a nurse on the payroll. Her husband's waist-deep with the ponies, and he's about to be cracked open like a Maine lobster by our bookie. My guess is that if she's reminded of her husband's 'status' within our community, she can find some bleach or kerosene to quietly stick in the bastard's IV . . ."

"Perfect," Rick responded serenely.

And there it was: Jus had just, for the first time, witnessed a murder contract being ordered by his uncle. He felt an intoxicating thrill surge through his entire body." At the time, neither Jus nor Uncle Rick could have had any idea that, years later, this "interest" in Rick's vocation would play an outsize role in Justin's occupational success. Practical and lucrative.

By the time Jus was thirty-eight, he was one of the youngest and most successful partners that Boston's prestigious Kensington & Pratt law firm had ever seen.

He was also The Hub's youngest and most unsuspected assassin-for-hire.

And as tough as it might be to believe, Jus was a pacifist. Although murder was his vocation, he practiced it *only* on those who "deserved it." Not that he fancied himself some real-life *Dexter*, but he was indeed a fan of the show, and Jus and the protagonist shared many of the same philosophies.

Jus certainly did not need the ancillary income that came from hits, but he used that capital to fund his philanthropic endeavors. His major benefactors were the Isabella Stewart Gardner Museum and the Dana–Farber Cancer Institute. He remembered the painful memories of his kid brother, Zack, who spent several months in Boston Children's Hospital with terminal leukemia. He sat for hours next to Zack's bed, totally incapable of anything that could serve to end his brother's suffering and return him to good health. All he could do was try to be the strong big brother, yet he was barely old enough to know that "goodbye" would be his final word to his beloved sibling.

Jus hated feeling powerless.

In the final hours of Zack's tragic life, Zack held Jus's hand while various family members incessantly wandered in and out of the hospital room, as if they had firm intentions to stay though they always seemed to find some feeble reason why they needed to return to the hallway.

Jus steadfastly remained.

As the sun finally gave up and relinquished her hope to the dark Boston night, and as Zack was falling more and more into unconsciousness, Jus felt that the time had come to address his ailing brother one last time. "Zack, man," he said softly, with a faltering voice. "Not sure if you understand me. I just want to say that your fight . . . your relentless battle . . . is what will carry both our souls, going forward. I wish I could make it go away. Whatever spirit, or god, or voodoo/hoodoo did this to you, I would strike back with a vengeance . . .

"Zack, I will love you forever, and I'll never forget the sounds of your laughter, your screams of joy at bad jokes, and your horrendous Fisher-Price xylophone playing . . ."

Justin wept.

After much suffering, Zack finally passed at the ripe old age of nine. It changed Jus. The losses that Jus had endured during his relatively short life had stripped him of much of his hope for humanity. Survival became the only option.

And so Justin McGee commenced a two-front war. A lifelong battle between himself and the world around him. And there only could remain one victor.

The money that went to the art museum was important to Jus because it symbolized a piece of humanity that he was trying to hold onto. He was obsessed with the urban myth that Whitey Bulger orchestrated the theft in the wee hours of March 18, 1990, when two thieves disguised as Boston Police officers talked their way into the facility and proceeded to tie up the guards before making off with thirteen paintings worth more than $500 million. The loot included a Vermeer, a Manet, a Degas, and two Rembrandts—not a bad smash and grab score for a couple of lowly Boston hoods. Even the filthiest of Monte Carlo Eurotrash would be envious.

One night Jus was at a museum benefit when he was approached by a stranger in a dark blue blazer.

"Mr. McGee, may I have a moment of your time? My name is Mink."

Justin was startled, for he made every effort to keep the lowest of profiles.

"All right, Mink. Five minutes. Whatcha got?"

Mink looked around furtively, shuffling his feet, hesitating, trying to be sure they weren't overheard.

"So, Mink. What's the good word?"

Mink, while remaining quite taciturn, quickly responded, "Jus, we need help. We need help in a most profound way. We think that we're onto something when it comes to the Gardner Museum heist. There's a guy just outside of Hartford who claims that he has connections tied to the theft of the paintings, and we want him questioned and interrogated in the old-fashioned way."

Hmm, thought Jus.

"Mink, why the fuck would I care about a finder's fee on a bunch of glorified posters. No way. Not worth the risk."

Jus stepped back and repeated that he had no interest, but that for the proper fee he might find himself inclined to take on the job.

Mink stepped back and said, "Jus, it's the gig of a lifetime. There's the reward money, and anyway it's a chance to do the right thing. Please consider giving this . . . due diligence."

"Hey, Mink, why the hell should I trust you when you've sold your soul to several other projects? It might be more interesting for me to go it alone without any so-called help from servants like yourself."

Jus received no reply.

The Next Day

Justin always found it difficult to park near Federal Street in downtown. Patience had never been his strong suit.

He finally found a pay lot that miraculously had some space left during the middle of the day, and he flipped the attendant an extra pair of twenties to situate his Maserati as far away as possible from the "madding crowd."

Jus got out and checked the side-view mirror to make sure that he looked respectable, but not too slick. When he paid his weekly visit to the Boston Big Brothers Big Sisters office, he didn't want to appear too fancy or pretentious. Some of his suits cost more than some of these kids' parents made in a month.

He walked into 75 Federal, and said hello to Katrina at the desk, who knew him very well and actually had a bit of a crush on the clandestine assassin. Jus was well accustomed to this kind of attention.

"Hello, Attorney McGee," she said, smiling brightly. "So nice to see you again."

To which he sincerely replied, "I'm only Attorney McGee at the office or in the courtroom. When I travel in the civilized world, I like to be called just plain old Justin."

"Fair enough . . . Justin. Leon's been waiting for you. He's so excited about your outing. He says that you're going to do something special with him today."

Jus replied, "I always try. . . Such a great kid."

Just then Leon emerged from the rather dark hallway with a beaming smile and immediately gave Justin a hug.

"What are we doing today, Mr. McGee?"

"Leon, I've told you. My name is Justin. Just like yours is Leon. I don't call you Mr. Adams, do I?"

Leon was indeed a great kid. He did really well in school. While Justin had never met his parents, through the Big Brothers program he learned that they were indeed a very solid, hard-working couple, and they greatly valued the few hours that Justin could spend with their son, showing him a world that perhaps he would never be able to see and appreciate without a bit of assistance.

"Okay, my friend. You're not going to need a coat today, but just grab a sweatshirt to bring along, if you have one with you."

At that, Leon ran the reverse route and got ready for his adventure.

A few minutes later, they found themselves in Justin's car heading west along the Mass Pike.

"Justin, where are we going?"

"It's a really fun surprise, Leon. Fun surprises are great gifts, and ones that are rarely given."

After traveling on both the Mass Pike and then Route 128 North, Justin pulled into Hanscom Field in Lexington and spoke to the attendant, who was awaiting their arrival.

"Attorney McGee," the man said, "your chopper is right over there, on the left. Your pilot is waiting."

Leon's eyes went wide. He had no idea what was happening.

"Justin, what's a 'chopper'?"

"You'll see, buddy."

They parked the Maserati in an out-of-the-way corner, as Justin always did, and walked across the tarmac to greet a man in a jumpsuit cradling a helmet under one arm.

"I'm Justin McGee. And this," he said, gesturing toward the boy beside him, "is my little brother Leon. Thank you so much for hosting us today."

"My pleasure," said the pilot, shaking hands with both of them. "I'm Captain Dan Callahan. Retired US Air Force. I'm confident that you'll enjoy the show. And without further ado . . ."

Leon freaked a bit when Captain Callahan pointed to a helicopter that was already warming up about 100 feet away.

"Justin, we're going to ride in *that*?"

"Yeah, Leon. We won't be too long. I have a feeling you'll love it."

Within minutes they had climbed aboard and buckled themselves into their seats. Soon the engine was roaring and the rotor blades spun faster and faster. Then, with an almost imperceptible shudder, the whirlybird rose and left the confines of terra firma.

They passed with a nice slow buzz over the timeless fields and farms of towns like Lincoln and Concord. From above, if one looked away from the cars and commercial sites, it truly hadn't changed in two hundred years.

Leon, speechless, pressed his face against the 'copter window. Jus could swear that he noticed a speck of drool on the sparkling glass.

To see Leon so happy rekindled whatever warmth was left in Justin's heart. He leaned back in his seat, stared at the blazing late-summer sun, and greeted it with a graceful and grateful smile.

Chapter 3

Captain Caleb Frost

Caleb would freelance whenever he could, for he certainly
needed the money. He often got referrals from a charter-captain friend
of his in Fort Lauderdale. Caleb checked in with a call.

After the fifth ring, a deep voice said, "Hello?"

"Hey, Captain Tommy! It's Caleb up here in Boston. How are
things in the Sunshine State? Business booming? Got a room for an
extra deckhand next winter?"

There was a long pause before Tommy boomed back, "Hey Caleb!
Great to hear from ya, but I'm friggin' pissed at the moment, so I'm
not my usual charming self. Got a real problem with today's charter."

"What's the matter, T.?" asked Caleb.

"I'm just pissed. I'm friggin' eight miles east of Key Largo
with this group who just won't goddamned listen to the captain's
instructions . . ."

Caleb knew all about guests like that. They charter a vessel, and for
one rum-soaked afternoon they feel as though they own it.

"Yeah, Tom, I understand. I've had those groups onboard. What
are they, smokin' dope?"

"No, no," replied a frustrated Captain Tommy. "No reef or anything. They just won't do as I ask. You see, I have a group of forty
women in their early thirties. Some kind of bachelorette thing or
whatever . . ."

Caleb thought to himself, *And this prick is complaining?*

Tommy continued, "Yeah, so I told them over and over: 'Fine. You can keep the tops off, but you must! You *must* keep your damned bottoms on!' And they friggin' refuse! Coast Guard will have my ass if they pull us over. I can't have that!"

Caleb was now firmly convinced that the salty spray had officially rotted out Captain Tommy's brain, in case there was ever was any question. "Well, T.," he said, smiling to himself. "Sounds like you have your hands full this afternoon. Hey, who's crewing for you?"

Tommy responded, "Oh, you know the usual. Deke and Dew-Man. Great guys, but they are no friggin' help! These broads keep getting lost on the boat and they keep draggin' Deke and Dew down below to help them find the galley and ladies' facility. My guys should be helping me navigate the vessel, but they're too damn busy navigating these chicks below deck to help them find their way around. Not sure why it's taking those two so long to give simple directions. At least the guys are being accommodating to the guests. I'll have to make sure I give them a decent cut of the tip."

"Yeah, Tommy. They seem like they're all about the guests. Good for your team." It was all Caleb could do to not burst out laughing.

Shit. . . Caleb loved and respected Tommy, but he did not feel the least bit of sympathy.

Chapter 4

Trav and McGill

The bloated rusty horn of the North Shore commuter ferry signaled to all around her that she was about to enter the harbor channel and was asking for neither permission nor invitation.

Trav and McGill preferred taking the ferry, especially on Friday afternoons, for they could pretend that they were not just nautical wannabe versions of the same ants who were simultaneously stuck and white-knuckle-wrapped on Route 1 North.

"Listen," said Travis MacDonald, then pausing to drain his third haul from the flask. "Nobody has sex with the masseuse—the hand ain't dealt that way. Odds are better that you'd draw a three-eyed jack."

"Kid, I couldn't script it better if I was named friggin' Neil Simon—trust me, it happened," responded McGill.

As old college friends often do when the opportunity arises, Trav and McGill talked over drinks while unabashedly attempting to one-up each other after yet another uneventful and less-than-satisfying day of peddling all things financial on the sea of open hands that is known as Boston's Financial District.

These two could have inspired a film combining *Groundhog Day* and *O Brother, Where Art Thou?*

Both were steaming toward the age of forty, and while these "cerebral" *tête-à-têtes* had become less frequent, they were nonetheless still important. Although both former roommates were quite successful in a monetary sense, nobody would have accused them of pulling off the Gardner Museum heist or orchestrating the Manhattan Project.

"C'mon," said Trav, "I'm a firm subscriber to the theory that there's 'no sex in the champagne room.' How did it all go down?"

After a not-so-pregnant pause during which McGill simultaneously chomped on an ice cube and ripped his second cocktail napkin into half-inch pieces, he mumbled, "I simply asked her . . ."

"What! You just *asked* her?"

"Yeah, Trav. I just asked her. Seek and ye shall find. She had these brown eyes and molasses skin, and the result was resoundingly . . . in the affirmative."

Trav picked up his fortification and stole a haul, then said, "That's the stuff ya read in Guccione's damned "Forum"—not sure that I'm buying what ya gots hanging off the barrow . . ."

Every sentence seemed to end with an unnecessarily elongated sigh, immediately followed by the proverbial "Fuck it . . ."

Off the port-side stern, a seagull hovered in the wind, awaiting some Friday-afternoon-and-already-buzzed wit to toss him a soggy French fry.

McGill noticed the bird and thought to himself, *What if those good-for-nothing flying rats were handed squeegees? Could they make a living at the South Station traffic snarl?*

These were the mind-blowing philosophical questions that really fried their circuit boards at the end of each week. These two wastes of oxygen truly felt as though they were holding court at the Acropolis during the heyday, or at least outside some flitty coffee shop on Brattle Street.

Still admiring the mindless flying sea-chicken, Trav remarked, "Hey, Gilly—imagine that, when it's all over, you and I would only be remembered for shitting on someone's head?"

Even the always-quick-with-the-answers McGill had to pause at that one. He took a wave of ocean spray across his half-closed eyes, and then sighed, "What makes you think that we won't?"

Promises had been made to McGill and Trav. Promised that if you eked out a B+ average, didn't knock up a cheerleader, and ate your green vegetables, then life would deliver endless gifts: cars, boats, pretty wives, and the answers to all of life's questions.

Thus far, at least, they had at least been rewarded with cars, boats, and pretty wives.

Jester Chauncey, CEO of Shea & Rizzo Securities

"Vera, please ask McGill and Trav to come in for a brief meeting. Actually, don't ask . . ."

Trav and McGill were nervous as they entered Jester's palatial office—they felt the mental duress.

Trav wasted no time. "Mr. Chauncey," he said, "we did nothing wrong. Damn stock as a start-up as overvalued to begin with. Mickey and I were just spotting an opportunity that would help the firm. There was no malice. Just trying to make a buck for all of us."

Jester said nothing.

"We're extremely scared of the D.A.'s office coming after us," Trav added hastily. "Bottom line: yes, it was a classic pump and dump. Nonetheless, the stock recovered and nobody really got hurt. As you know yourself, money just moves from one side of a screen to another. Nothing is ever truly created or destroyed."

Jester finally felt the need to interject. "Guys," he said. "You are great ambassadors for the firm, even though you could pack your brains together in a Disney World fanny pack—a small one. If you were on a golf course, your tee shots would slice away two hundred yards and you'd never get out of the weeds."

He paused to let this sink in, then went on. "Let's remember, boys. We are here for one reason only: to make money for S&R Securities. Yeah, if you have to cut a corner or two, shit, that's America, but in the end you just have to keep your dilated pupils set on the goal. Right? Look, I hired both of you 'cause I thought you had some feeble amount of, dare I say 'talent,' and I still see potential. I see . . . well . . . a bit of me at your age. The worst thing you can do is not attack this situation like a honey badger ripping into the sternum of a so-called unbeatable king cobra, only to skin him alive while he's still erect and thinks he's in charge."

He sighed and lowered his voice. "My advice is to keep your eyes on the opportunities, and keep your faces out of what's below those singing sirens you like to cavort with, and just focus on the matter at hand."

Trav and McGill understood that this was a reprieve.

Jester shooed them out of his office, growling, "And whatever you do, stay away from the friggin' D.A.'s office!"

Justin and Meyer, circa 1983

"You gonna finish that fuckin' Yodel?" asked a six-year-old Meyer of the boy who would be his best friend for life, Justin McGee.

"*I heard that!*" shrieked their first-grade teacher, Mrs. Drew. ("Rhymes with *shrew*," the boys liked to say behind her back.)

As the boys tried to stifle their snickers, she demanded, "Where did you learn such horrible language!"

To which Meyer replied with the straightest of faces, "You and HBO!"

The old hen just shook her head and thought to herself, *Future of the world, my fat ass . . .*

Meyer had always been precocious and well beyond his years as a child. As his teacher berated them, he quietly wondered why, if she hated the kids so much, had she taught for so long. He thought to himself that she would be much happier working inside one of those trick mirrors at Revere Beach—the ones where people laughed because they could make a Natalie Portman look-alike resemble Mrs. Drew. *It wouldn't even be work for her*, he thought, and wondered if she wouldn't be much happier making people smile . . .

That was the memory that stuck in Meyer's brain as he waited for the medic after the roadside bomb went off in Iraq.

All he could remember was walking down the road. Every path looked the same, for there was no landscaping, no friendly smiles from a neighbor watering the grass. He remembered that somebody had a boom box hanging off the starboard side of an Allied jeep, cranking out AC/DC. Nothing could get the troops fired up and engaged quite like side two of *Back in Black*. Sometimes it was tough to get them motivated, since most of them, in their hearts, didn't believe they should be there in the first place.

Only barren visions, and subsequent empty thoughts.

All was quiet that morning as Meyer and his platoon wandered down the pathway, knowing that today, pretty much like the previous several outings, wasn't going to render much in the way of productivity.

And then, all of a sudden—*K'BLAM!*

Meyer kept looking forward, as his training demanded. In the face of enemy fire, a good soldier persevered. He just kept marching—to where, he had no clue.

Marching and marching . . .

Until he realized that both of his legs were attached to his body by nothing more than sinews, and that he was horizontal to the earth and coughing up sand.

The medics bravely ran over to him and quickly hauled Meyer into the "buggy."

His legs felt like overcooked angel-hair pasta. He feared the worst—and for good reason. The only thing his mind, which at the moment was a separate entity from his body, could ask was: "Is this all worth it?"

Meyer was losing a lot of blood, but the medical staff stuck to their business—they were pros. They were not going to lose this brave man. Not on their watch.

Several surgeries and God-knows-how-many treatments later, Meyer finally awoke and realized that the use of his precious legs was gone forever. He was still in shock, and yet his tidal pain slowly began to ebb, only to give into bitterness.

Meyer would never be the same man again, and in some twisted way, nor did he ever want to be.

Years later, he would receive a new mission order. This time, though, it was from within.

Chapter 5

Justin and Darby

"You look like you just ran through the spin cycle—twice," quipped Darby McBride as he picked the splinters out of his tender gums—the result of a painful habit of chomping on toothpicks in his vain effort to forget the coffin nails, a.k.a. unfiltered Camels.

His doctor had advised him eighteen months earlier to jettison the three-pack-a-day habit, or else just chain himself to a leftover piece of concrete from the Big Dig and jump over the Tobin Bridge rail—that way he'd be saving his health insurance provider a lot of money, and the Mass General medical staff a lot of precious time and aggravation.

Darby took the advice but resented the doc's delivery, for his apathetic eyes simply said, *Do whatever you want—you're just another dead white-trash mick and the city will endure, and there'll be plenty more like you, as history clearly shows . . .*

Darby wondered if there was anyone so annoyingly smug as a once-nerdy medical student turned omniscient genius . . .

Jus finally broke the awkward silence. "Business has been kinda slow, Darb. A few more of these runs, and I'll have to find a job like yours."

Darby did indeed ply a unique trade. In the wake of the vacuum created by the implosion of the Angiulo crime family, as well as the slow disappearance of the Winter Hill Gang, Boston had set the stage for guys like Darby McBride to reconfigure the underworld—or better yet, the "new world" of sole proprietorships—and indeed they sprang up like wild mushrooms throughout the city. The "new economy" was not reserved for the dribbling snot-noses on Route 128.

Not a bad gig. American entrepreneurship at its best. Like so many of this new breed, Darby spent his Sundays at neither St. Brigid's nor the Myopia Hunt Club.

Looking down on the well-worn, barnacle-capped docks of the Boston waterfront as he was negotiating a shipment receipt, Darby's mind would often wander to his days as a young South Boston raga-muffin. He and his fellow "no-faith-in-any-future" gang would hang out in alleyways while trading curses and throwing dice. To say that they would share their daydreams would be an outright lie, for they were certainly devoid of any. What this South Boston version of *Our Gang* did possess, though, was a wide-eyed infatuation with the older neighborhood guys who never seemed to work, but always had more money and swagger than anyone within five miles of L Street. There was some buzz around the neighborhood that they were engaged in illegal activities. For some reason, however, not only did they never get arrested, but when a police cruiser would pass by, the cop and Mahoney, the leader of the "older guys," would kind of smile at one another.

Darby was inspired by the memory of one incident in particular.

Mahoney's kid sister Maureen was a doll of a lass who maintained A+ grades and stayed away from any neighborhood shenanigans. One raw, drizzly afternoon, as she was walking home from school, a local hood named Sully, who always had eyes on all of the young South Boston girls, and who never really fit into any crew, was driving along in his black Chevrolet Chevelle. He was stoned. When he spotted Maureen on the sidewalk, he pulled over and offered her a ride home. She politely declined, and kept walking.

Sully was undeterred, though, and slowly, at no-wake speed, he cruised along beside her, pressing his offer. "C'mon, Mo! Get in and we'll go for a ride!"

To which Maureen responded, "No thank you, Mr. Sullivan. I'm quite fine. I'm just a few blocks away from home."

There are defining mistakes in life. Defining moments that one would forever wish to have back. Face it—everyone has them.

For Sully, such a moment came on a foggy, drizzly afternoon when he would make a foolish and fateful decision.

As he drove slowly along, still trying to cajole Maureen Mahoney to ride with him, Sully thought back to his childhood in Southie.

His mom, a pious Irish Catholic, had one all-surpassing aspiration for her only son—that he become an altar boy. Sully would show up at the Gate of Heaven Church on Saturdays in order to prepare and rehearse for the very well-attended Sunday services. One such attendee was always Sully's mom, and he wanted nothing more than to make her proud and to stay in her favor. Sully's dad rarely spoke to him or anyone else for that matter, and usually it was with a pronounced, Jameson-induced slur followed by a savage and shaky backhand.

One typical Saturday, Sully went to the rectory to meet with Father Leary, for whom he would be performing Mass the next morning. Father Leary was always very upbeat and cheerful, despite all of the rumors that, financially, his church was sailing on troubled waters.

Father Leary said, "Mr. Sullivan, would you please come over here and make sure that we have enough hosts ready to distribute during communion tomorrow."

Sully always complied unhesitatingly with the priest's orders, for he wanted nothing more than to make his mother proud. He went over and began a quick count of the communion wafers, using a plastic fork in order to avoid touching them with his unworthy hands. By his rough count, he figured that they possessed about 300 communion hosts, which would be ample for a normal Sunday Mass. He then reported back to the old priest. "Father, I think that we have enough to handle tomorrow's service. We should be fine. If you think that we need more, I'll be more than happy to get some more from the parish store."

"No, thank you, Mr. Sullivan," said Father Leary. "I appreciate your service and concern for our parish's success and vibrancy. Tell me, Sully, do you ever go by another name? Perhaps a more proper way to address you?"

"No, Father," responded the boy, slightly embarrassed. "I like being called Sully—everyone in the neighborhood knows it and that's the only name they put to my face."

"I see," responded Father Leary. "Have you ever played a pinball machine?"

Sully immediately brightened and said, "Oh yes, one time. It was really fun! Why, do you know where one is?"

Father looked at the naive young Sully and beckoned him, "Walk right this way . . ."

For a moment Sully was so lost in this memory that he could barely even see Maureen Mahoney on the sidewalk beside him, but then he shook his head loose of daydreaming about the past and popped the Chevelle onto the crumbling concrete curb. He was amazed at how the demons of the past could intrude themselves so vividly into his present thoughts.

He jumped out of his car, grabbed Maureen, and semi-gently guided her to the passenger-side door.

Maureen, reflexively polite, barely resisted and found herself in the shotgun seat of Sully's black Chevy. She held onto her schoolbooks like a life preserver, while her right leg shook uncontrollably.

Sully jumped back behind the wheel, peeled out, and headed toward the beach.

There, Sully played Romeo. "Maureen," he said as soon as he'd stopped the car, "I've always thought that you were so beautiful. I've always admired how you've turned into a woman right before the world's eyes."

Maureen sat stock-still in fear and horror. "Mr. Sullivan," she said falteringly. "Please just let me walk back home. I promise to keep my mouth shut, but I just want to go home."

As Sully gingerly touched her knee, Maureen bit his arm just as hard as a wounded mako shark off of Nantucket. As Sully screamed, as much in surprise as in pain, she threw open the Chevelle's creaky door and then ran like hell. Her older brother would have been proud.

Sully sat in shock. First, because his arm throbbed. Second, because he knew what he had just put into motion . . .

Sully kept a low profile for the next few days. He kept the old Chevelle in the garage, not that it would serve as a deterrent to Mahoney, but keeping the car out of sight gave him a sense of security—in this case, a false sense of security. In his arrogance, there was a significant part of him that thought maybe the young chick would keep her mouth shut, out of some twisted version of Catholic guilt. But the rest of him knew that it was a matter of time.

When Sully wasn't high and needed to relax, he loved to shoot pool quietly at the neighborhood pool hall, Sheppard's. On this particular day, he was having a hard time keeping his eyes focused on the cue ball as he made a feeble attempt to clear the table. Then, as Sully was sinking a nine-ball in the corner pocket, the din of the Sheppard's crowd suddenly grew low.

Mahoney had arrived, alone and looking quite calm. No entourage. Nothing threatening.

"Sully," he said, "you and I need to have a bit of a talk. Don't worry. Nothing elaborate. I'm not mad. Trust me—I've made my share of mistakes. I just wanna understand if my kid sister is or is not embellishing her version of last week's events."

Sully began to shake. "Mahoney," he said hastily, "I was high. I didn't know what I was—"

Mahoney put his hand out and stopped him. "I understand, Sully. I totally understand. I'm your old friend. I just want to know what went down so that I can properly coach my promiscuous kid sister, for she obviously led you on in order to evoke such behavior on your part. Did she flash her frilly panties as you drove by?"

Sully wasn't sure where this was going. Yet he really had no choice other than to listen politely and do as he was told. "Mahoney," he said,

"I thought that she wanted to hang out. I thought that she wanted to spend time. That's all. It seemed like she wanted to. I swear."

Mahoney instructed him to walk out the back door of the pool hall, where Mahoney's was parked, and to keep his mouth shut.

As Mahoney guided him out through the back lot, Sully noticed a few of Mahoney's crew surrounding a very innocent-looking Maureen.

They walked forward as Mahoney said to her, "Hey, kid sis, is this the gentleman who so generously offered you a ride home last week?"

Maureen hesitated for a solid thirty seconds. To Sully, it seemed like a thousand years.

"Y-Y-Yes, big brother . . . ," the young girl finally responded.

"Thanks, sis—that was very kind of him. Please thank him."

Maureen looked confused and remained quiet.

"Maureen, please say thank you for the offer of a ride."

Maureen was as frightened as Sully and said, "Mr. Sullivan, thank you for offering me a ride. I was just very close to home and I didn't need it."

Sully saw where this was going and capitulated, "No problem, anytime . . ."

And that would be the last time Sully would ever be seen in South Boston. Well, almost the last time . . .

Fast-forward twelve hours as the Boston Police approached the car. They found that Sully's Chevelle had a cinder block on the accelerator, yet the vehicle was in park with the emergency brake fully engaged. The powerful engine revved and smoked like a sleeping white dragon, yet there was no driver at the wheel.

When the police popped the hood, they found poor Sully literally sizzling against a red-hot engine block. He looked like an overdone sirloin at a Fourth of July cookout where the chef was buzzed and forgot to turn down the gas. There was no blood, of course—it had all been cooked away . . .

To Darby, this story epitomized what real "power" meant, and from a young age that's what he would aspire to.

His memories often would meander back to his dad, a dockworker, who came home every day smelling of sweat and Jameson. He would grunt at Darb's mom and then find somewhere to pass out.

Darb knew that there had to be another way. While some young boys revered and idolized their fathers, to Darby his dad was just an example of what *not* to do in life. He wanted more and better—like the "older guys."

To the new breed of entrepreneurs, like Justin, Darb's old-school reputation was the stuff of cherished folklore. It was once said that anytime you double-crossed or, heaven forbid, stole from Darby McBride, you would earn yourself one nice slash across your Achilles tendon. It was speculated that Darby did this so that when you dealt with him in the future, perhaps at a waterfront loading dock while you wore a T-shirt, Darb could tell by the number of lashes that you sported how badly you had pissed him off in the past.

For Darby, it was like a Woods Hole geek tagging a great white off of Monomoy Island. Rumor had it that Darb was about to launch an app that could track the movements and whereabouts of anyone that he branded. Of course, this would not be a free application and certainly it would come with a price tag.

Indeed, free trade and capitalism were alive and well in the birthplace of our nation, despite the presence of both a socialist governor and a socialist US president. They could set all the controls and regulations that they wanted, but in this part of the world, only one system would prevail, and it was as old as the birth of the city.

Jus left Darby in an especially foul mood, which was not difficult to accomplish. Sure, he relished the rush and the challenge, but as he got on in years, the concept of self-inflicted forced retirement hung from his neck like a dead albatross.

Fuck.

Jus loved Darby like an uncle, but he feared him as life's turnstile. Back in the day, when Darb and the gang wanted to "off" Casey O'Casey, or some other mick that got out of line, it was pretty easy.

First of all, the rules were easier: you did not get out of line.

Lest you did, well . . . they had to open up another chapter in the book and blow off the dust.

Casey O' had a shipment coming in with Darby. This was an easy job, and Darb couldn't wait to move this small shipment of some "brown" and a few handguns. Not a big score, he thought—*Just get me home and in bed in one piece.* Back in the day, the jobs were so much simpler. Darb now had to find a new place in a new world.

The fifty-foot trawler pulled into Boston Harbor, and Darby's crew began unloading the evening's "pull."

It was so much easier back then.

Just easier . . .

While he still loved the hunt, he felt the kind of frustration a man in his mid-sixties feels when he spends ten minutes looking for his reading glasses, only to eventually look in the mirror and find them on his head.

Perhaps it was the loneliness of his occupation that, like a relentless wind, was beginning to wear away his stone face. His union-delegate business was booming, but that gave him nothing like the satisfaction offered by his moonlighting gig—and even *that* was beginning to lose its flavor.

Chapter 6

Justin and Uncle Rick

Jus certainly never aspired to become an assassin—who does? For Jus, it took a profound catalyst that rocked him to the core. When he was about fourteen years old, he was walking downtown with his uncle as they made their usual rounds. The day was rather gray, with a strong, biting breeze. Uncle Rick always walked very fast, and Jus always struggled to keep up. He often wondered why Rick always seemed to be in such a hurry.

Jus was actually a little worried about his uncle that day, for he was unusually quiet. Not that Rick would ever be accused of being paid by the word, but today he seemed especially distracted and distant. Jus wondered if it had something to do with a phone conversation he had inadvertently overheard a couple of days earlier as his uncle was explaining to somebody that he felt that the time had come to retire.

That confused Jus, because even at such a young age, he thought that in order to retire you actually had to have something to retire *from*. He had no idea that Rick actually worked, for he never seemed to have to be anywhere in the morning, and he never mentioned anything about a job.

They crossed Main Street in order to head over to the jewelry store for their usual Saturday-morning visit, when a late-model sedan pulled up next to the sidewalk beside them. The greasy-looking, wiry guy in the passenger seat leaned out the window and said to Rick, "Excuse me. Do you know how to get to the train station?"

What happened next seemed to play out in slow motion. As Rick approached the car in order to give the man directions, said passenger fired five pieces of lead into Rick's stomach and chest.

The car's tires squealed as the assailants fled the scene. Jus never got the license-plate number, for he was having an out-of-body experience as he watched his uncle slowly buckle at the knees and fall to the pavement in a most unnatural contorted shape. Rick just stared into the sky and was silent. For one brief moment, he managed to turn his head and gave Jus a plastic glance and uttered, "Justin . . . ," and then he was still.

A crowd began to gather around, and people started screaming. Some of the bystanders recognized Rick, as he was quite well known within the community. A middle-aged woman stepped forward, yelling that she was a nurse, and she began trying to tend to the mortally wounded man. An elderly fellow immediately went to the pay phone to call for an ambulance, but he probably just should have called the hearse.

Jus didn't scream. He didn't cry. He stood silent and still, in a horrific state of shock. His body took on the color of alabaster. All he could think of was that his world had just been shattered, and that life would never be the same—if indeed he could ever live again at all.

Jus didn't hear the people screaming, nor was he aware of the approaching sirens. All he heard was the sound of a group of children playing in a park half a block away. They were yelling and laughing in the chilly afternoon. Their world was grand and filled with joy and possibilities. In their minds, the sun would never set and the night would never shatter the day.

The ambulance and police cruisers screeched to a halt, and the EMTs rushed to Rick's aid. But it was too late—Uncle Rick was already dead.

The police cordoned off the crime scene as the EMTs lifted Rick onto the gurney and slowly and quietly loaded him into the back of the ambulance.

One EMT asked Jus if he wanted to ride along, but Jus only stared at him and did not respond. The ambulance driver took this as a no, and they proceeded to leave the scene. Jus could only stare as the ambulance pulled away, leaving the most painful vapor trail. It was then that Jus caught a whiff of Rick's aftershave in the wind.

In that moment, Jus realized that the world was devoid of a soul and that life was not only short but fundamentally lacked any true meaning. He would exact his vengeance on those who selfishly snatched innocent lives and shattered their dreams.

Jus fired up his Maserati and pulled into unusually light traffic on Storrow Drive. He headed west, with the sleepy Charles River on his starboard side, and contemplated his future—if there would even be any future at all.

As his thoughts meandered, suddenly he was cut off by a Boston Cab, forcing Jus to slam on his brakes within a split second of an accident, which on Storrow Drive was as unique as seeing an alligator in the Everglades.

"Jack off!" screamed Jus as he leaned onto the fine Italian leather covering of his unusually loud horn. The cabbie slammed on his brakes and pulled over, while simultaneously making the mistake of motioning for Jus to do the same. Jus, of course took up the challenge and the two pulled into a parking area beside the Charles, with Jus ending up about a foot away from the beat-up taxi.

The cabbie got out with mouth blazing, for he was already fired up and pissed off about his business being down for the sixth consecutive month, due to slowly being eroded away by what he called the "Uber molesters."

Jus approached him. "Hey, dildo," he snarled. "Where'd you learn to drive? Kabul?"

The cab driver, not at all amused at being mistaken for an Afghani, responded, "Hey, buddy, I'm fuckin' Lebanese American, so don't give me that racist shit. Just 'cause you drive one of those fancy Ferraris doesn't mean you own the road. Go fuck yourself!"

Without another word, Jus slowly pulled out a recently acquired Glock to which he had a fondness.

His first instinct was to put two bullets in the driver's skull and leave him in the trunk with country music playing on the car's radio. But Jus was neither a murderer of civilians nor an animal, and this man, however annoying he might be at the moment, did not deserve to die.

Instead, Jus merely fired one shot into each of the taxi's back tires, quietly let his weapon cool, and slipped it back into his shoulder holster. The cabbie stood in shock, and Jus couldn't help but chuckle softly at the sight of the urine stain spreading down the man's left thigh.

"Now, Mr. Cab Man," Jus said. "My advice is to hand me your keys. Get into your taxi. Wait ten minutes after I pull away, which of course I will do while backing out of here so you don't see my license plate, and then you can call your dispatcher. Tell him you've been robbed. Take all of the cash that you have on you from tonight's fares and hide it somewhere in this park so that you can come and get it later. That way, they have nothing on you, and you get to keep the money instead of having to turn it over at the end of your shift. If you think you need better convincing for your boss, I'd be happy to put a bullet in your shoulder or your—"

The cabbie stopped him in mid-sentence. "No, no! The bullets in the tires are good enough. Please, just don't hurt me—I have children!"

"Great," replied Jus. "Then stash the money and buy them an ice cream tomorrow."

And with that, Jus backed his car away, and then pulled back onto Storrow Drive westbound.

Another good deed in the interest of the community . . .

Chapter 7

Jus, Darby, and Meyer

Darby McBride seemed unusually nervous as he stepped up and greeted Meyer and Jus at the bar at the Marriott Long Wharf.

Before Darb could toss out a few pleasantries (which for him normally amounted to a grunt and a "How the fuck are you?"), or even get himself seated, Justin stopped him. "What you stewin' on, Darb?"

To which Darb replied, "Well . . . Houston we have a problem."

Jus knew that this smelled of a real issue, for nothing rattled Darb.

All this while Meyer was as wide-eyed as a deer crossing Cape Cod's Route 6 at midnight.

Darb began, "Well, that hit that you did—"

Jus stopped him so abruptly that Meyer was afraid that he would actually smack Darb in the face, which unfortunately would have resulted in only one of the two "friends" leaving the bar vertically that afternoon.

"Darb," Justin interrupted. "That was *our* hit. You got paid as well."

Darb replied, "Well, unfortunately it turns out that Crasha was a niece of Don Cistulli, and, well . . . you know . . . not good."

Meyer feared that Justin was going to pull out the Glock at that very moment and end Darby McBride's sad semblance of a life.

"You fuckin' son of a bitch!" hissed Jus. "Are you out of your brain-dead, two-bit Irish mind?! Damn, you suck balls!"

Darby calmly retorted, "It was an oversight . . ."

Jus wasn't having it. "An oversight? You washed-up son of a bitch! So how many cement blocks is Cistulli gonna have ready for our off-shore fishing trip later today?"

"All right, Jus. Take it easy. What's done is done. Let's see if we can have a sit-down and try to make amends."

"What the F did you get Meyer and me into, you walking anachronism? Damn! It . . . it was *not* supposed to roll this way."

"You know what your problem is, Darb?"

Darb quietly replied, "No. What?"

"You don't *suck* enough!"

Darb brushed off the comment like he was dusting off a bit of lint.

"Jus, I do have one other job for you—if you're interested."

Jus merely rolled his eyes—even at his peak intensity he was always willing to listen, if it involved a hefty fee for service.

"You see, Jus, there's this really highfalutin bond analyst named Matilda Chong. She's known all around the world. Anyway, I was approached by a firm that needs her gone."

Darby paused before proceeding, confident now that he had Justin's attention. "She apparently is rather promiscuous in her private life," he went on, "and leads what you might call an alternative lifestyle—you know, deep female kisses and cast-iron dildos—and yet she suffers from an acute case of ego-driven Tourette's . . .

"Anyway, when she was in New York on business, she got caught up with the daughter of the North Korean consul, whom she met at some fancy UN party. Supposedly, the two made quite a tryst of it, but our target figured that it was more than just a road trip and was looking for some semblance of a relationship. Said Korean girl was in no way interested and just wanted a few days of sex, and so Matilda felt scorned.

"'Hell hath no fury,' quoth Billy Shakes. Anyway, Matilda—who was all bullshit—went back to Boston and began to high-profile downgrade all of the Korean father's company's debt instruments, and—"

Before Darby could go any further, Justin cut him off. "Wait a minute," he demanded. "Fuckin' wait, Darb. Are you asking me to take out Matilda Chong? Don't you think that I know about her? She's a legend in the investment world, not only in this town but literally worldwide. Our firm has done business with hers for years. Are you cutting your own hair and then rolling it up and smoking it?"

Darb took this in and then conceded, "Granted, she's all the shit, Jus. When this analyst talks, the street listens and they listen good."

Jus tilted his head back, took a huge breath and blew it out, then ran his fingers through his tired hair. "Darb," he inquired, "what the hell are you getting at? Don't tell me that you were hired by North Koreans to kill a marquee Boston investment chick. Are you crazy?"

"Yeah, Jus. I'm crazy. Crazy enough to split a $250,000 fee . . ."

To that Jus merely paused and stared at Darby for several seconds. Then he took another deep breath and continued. "That's a lotta dough, Darb, and I could use it—or more accurately, would love it." He took a sip of beer and then said in a low voice, "So how do I find her?"

Apparently, Jus' conscience had left briefly to powder its nose.

Darby leaned toward him, saying softly, "She lives in a mansion in Louisburg Square on Beacon Hill, and she goes for a long run every Sunday morning around seven. That's where you hit her."

Jus was unusually quiet for a long time before responding, "All right, Darb. But no more of these wacky one-offs. In this case, however, the cash would be fun for . . . stockpiling. Today is Thursday. I'll plan on the job for Sunday—I want to get this out of the way. To tell you the truth, I don't like this one at all, *and* I want to get fucking paid the next day."

"Don't worry," Darb responded. "You'll get your money, but it will take until mid-week."

Chapter 8

Jus and Matilda

Sunday approached and generously delivered a beautiful morning for a run. Matilda peeled off her silk pajamas and replaced them with the latest distance-running fashion, accented by sleek European sunglasses.

She looked nothing short of radiant.

Her neighbor, a downtown equity-fund manager out walking his dog, was trying desperately to keep from staring at Matilda's Aphrodite-like body. Little did he suspect that she played for the other team—which, actually, had he known, would have gotten him even more aroused. Seeing her stretch her body was certainly better than picking up dogshit on his daily neighborhood canine trek.

Matilda began her run down the hill and immediately headed for the park along the Charles.

Justin, meanwhile, had just finished setting up shop on the Arthur Fiedler footbridge next to the Charles River. He remembered from childhood hearing stories about the legendary Fiedler, who, supposedly, enjoyed a cocktail or two while conducting the "1812 Overture."

Good for him, thought Jus.

This was going to have to be a quick operation. There were some people around but, fortunately, nobody using the bridge.

Jus waited.

About ten minutes later, the perfect figure of Matilda Chong materialized on the opposite side of the street near the entrance to the Hatch Shell, a performing space beside the Charles.

Jus had his work cut out for him, for Matilda was in impeccable shape and kept up a brisk pace. He calculated that he had only about ten seconds to complete this job before getting noticed.

As she rounded a curve on the footpath, Jus pulled his weapon of the day out of his duffel bag, positioned himself on the handrail, and aimed, staring into the scope.

A flock of birds fled a nearby tree as if in anticipation of the impending chaos.

Suddenly, Matilda stopped dead in her tracks, startling Jus.

She stooped down to pat a young golden retriever, whose coat glowed like the Yellow Brick Road. The dog's owner, a gorgeous blonde, was now directly in between Jus and his target. Jus wondered whether Matilda was actually interested in the canine, or just wanted an excuse to strike up a conversation with the owner.

Either way, it was messing up Jus's line of fire. He never violated his personal rule: No collateral damage.

The two perfectly attractive women exchanged pleasantries and began a conversation.

Jus felt the sweat on his temple, as he had little time remaining before he had to leave the bridge, lest he attract suspicion.

Finally, after the seconds seemed to drip like icicles, the two beauties both petted said animal and each went her own way. Jus wanted to take out Matilda before she reached her stride.

It was then that Jus did what he does best.

Matilda's brilliant brain was removed from her body, which actually kept running for a step or two, like a decapitated hen that doesn't realize her time is up. (Ironic, because that's what her dad had sold back in the marketplace in Beijing.)

It was a perfect shot, and within a few seconds Jus had the weapon back in the duffle bag and was walking swiftly down the north side of the bridge toward Beacon Street, where Meyer was waiting with his idling van.

All in a day's work, thought Jus.

And in the end, he hardly gave the matter another thought at all. Jus was a walking dichotomy. With equal intensity, he thought about everything and, simultaneously, nothing.

Trav and McGill: Office of Shea & Rizzo Securities

Trav and McGill did not exactly have corner offices at Goldman Sachs. Sure, they did well financially, but they plied their trade at a particularly low-rent firm. S&R was a second-tier outfit at best, as evidenced by their tacky decor in the lobby, which had not been updated since Saddam marched into Kuwait. The plastic spider plant hanging from the ceiling complemented the faded Monet print in a dust-covered fake brass frame.

McGill was on the phone. "Yeah," he was saying, "so's I'm sitting at the office—manager yells at us to move about ten thousand shares of some 'guppy' who's barely managing to hold on to their office space on friggin' 128.

"Smells to me like a glorified pump and dump," he went on, "a dance as old as that broad down in Accounting. You know—the one who could be a stunt double for Jabba the Hutt? Yet I digress. . . Our parent firm got stuck bringing this hound public because our illustrious CEO, Mr. Chauncey, had one too many 'due diligence' meetings with said company's chief stockholder. It seems that Daddy left her with too many shares to count, and an existence that rendered too few brain cells with which to function. What a mess. . . Broads . . ."

McGill continued, "So here we are, a few months later, and the damned DA's office is up our ass and threatening to bring in the US Attorney's squadron of hypocrites. They're accusing us of monkeying around with the stock price in order to overly benefit said dog. The firm is named BeamTech. Stupid-ass name. . . You ask me, they're a bunch of ankle-grabbers. . . Soccer in the summer . . . Dungeons & Dragons all winter . . ."

Chapter 9

Capt. Caleb Frost

One thing that Caleb had learned early in life is that the damned wind is stubborn. Later in life, he learned that the only entity with more resolve than the wind was his own will.

Caleb was the proud owner and pilot of a fishing boat named *Coney Island Whitefish*, a rather weather-beaten but mightily New England–sturdy—a semi-custom Young Brothers, Down East–style vessel. With a full-fuel-tank weight of almost nine tons, and just over forty feet in length and a plump thirteen and a half on her beam, the *Whitefish* could handle pretty much anything Mother Nature could mercilessly dish out. Moreover, pushing her along was an unleashed diesel beast which made her unpredictably fast!

What appeared to be a normal Sunday morning fishing charter with a half-dozen customers who were certain to keep getting their damned fishhooks stuck in their thumbs, turned out to possess a few more moving parts than any of his crew could ever imagine. *Gotta pick up the bait* was monopolizing his ever-churning mind.

If, even for only one second, Caleb could envision a "land" job, he might have used his seafaring credentials at leisure. Instead, it's running charters by necessity and having to occasionally remark, "Yes, Dr. Grimm, I shall change the direction of that pesky northeast blow, lest you spill your ninth Heineken . . ." Yes, instead, it's offshore with charlatan anglers who were pretending to themselves that this trip was not what it really was: a liberating day away from their wives.

"At least I'm making a living" was the mantra that Caleb recited to himself with as much enthusiasm as a fourth-grade homeroom reciting the Pledge of Allegiance on a late-June morning with two days to go until summer vacation . . .

Captain Caleb learned the hard way that, while the tuna offshore tend to disappear on a whim, the mortgage company is a bit more steadfast.

A bale of "bait" is extremely heavy. Yet it can be oh-so-light to the touch, and sweet to the smell.

The stress and anxiety rendered by the whole scene cast Caleb into a reminiscence about a certain childhood incident . . .

When Caleb was in his early teens, he left his house one night with his surfcasting fishing gear and walked down to a spit of sand near where the stripers had been biting voraciously. He set his seven-foot rod into a sand spike and proceeded to try and wake up one of the live eels that he had put on ice in his fishing bucket. He loved using live eels as bait, for they performed a ballet-like dance that no striped bass could easily resist.

He hooked the first eel through the eye and then rolled the hook through the mouth. One might find that cruel, but it was a means of survival hundreds of years ago, and anyhow, said eel was already on his way out, due to hypothermia.

Caleb grabbed his long surf rod and cast the bait about fifty yards into the calm black sea. Then he commenced with the activity that all true fisherman do best. He waited . . .

He noticed subtle movements on the tip of the long rod as the eel swam in various directions in a feverous desire to return to the depths of the ocean.

Not tonight, thought young Caleb.

All of a sudden, the pole doubled over with a contorted bend, and Caleb grabbed it from the sand spike and steeled himself for the ensuing fight with a lunker striped bass.

He let the bass run for a few seconds and then twisted tight on the drag mechanism so that the hook would set deeply in the fish's mouth, thus ensuring against the age-old defensive move of the elusive New England striper.

With the line taut, Caleb began the fight as if the bell had rung and he was dancing in the ring with Marvin Hagler. He muscled the rod up in an arc motion and then reeled furiously on the way down, all the time keeping the line tight against the striper's mouth.

This dance battle lasted for about ten minutes when suddenly Caleb's young teenage body was starting to lose steam. He knew that needed to get into the water and get the fish close enough to shore to snag him by the gills and toss him onto the sand.

As Caleb waded into the strong current, he suddenly lost his footing on the silty bottom. As he slid into four feet of water, he somehow managed to kick off his rubber body waders, which were already nearly filled with water. If he had not been able to jettison said fishing apparel, he would have sunk like a stone and surely would have drowned.

With the waders off, he quickly grew cold, and sheer panic made him disoriented. In his frenzy he dropped the fishing pole and lost his eyeglasses. Without the luxury of eyesight he tried to swim, but with his glasses gone and the fog bank gradually engulfing him, he had no idea which direction would get him back to land.

Soon exhausted, he floated. Cold and in shock. And growing quickly colder.

As the current pulled him farther into the channel, he completely lost all sense of location and direction. Afloat in the freezing water, as aimless as a jellyfish in a North Atlantic tidal change, he thought of his life and his pending death doing what he loved. Despite his youth, Caleb was introspective by nature, but at the moment introspection was not a survival skill.

As he floated, he wondered whether he would see Jesus. He wondered whether he would encounter Mother Mary, who might render assistance, for his tender soul was too young to die such an untimely death by drowning.

In the end, though, by some miracle, he would meet neither Jesus nor Mary that day.

He suddenly noticed, about thirty yards away, a trawler that belonged to one of the old salts in the harbor. It swung listlessly on a rusty mooring, and the current was pulling him closer to it. Caleb knew that if he could just climb aboard he might be able to gather his wits and find his bearings.

As he approached, he found a last gasp of air and energy to breaststroke over to the transom, where there was a metal fitting of some sort that he could use as an impromptu swim ladder. With the last of his strength, he hoisted himself up onto the aft deck and then utterly collapsed in exhaustion and unconstrained tears.

He lay there for about ten minutes, regaining his breath and his thoughts, but his body temperature was still falling alarmingly. Even as an adolescent, Caleb possessed the maritime knowledge to know that, given the boat's position in the strong incoming tide, if he dove off the starboard side, he could reach land in about fifty yards.

He rose wearily to his feet and walked with an unsteady gait to the starboard side. He looked down at the water, and all his nearsighted eyes could take in was profound blackness. He knew that this was his only chance before he became so cold that he would be stricken with total immobility.

In his confused and shocked mind, he picked a direction and dove into the cold Atlantic. What was left of his adrenaline raged through his body as he feverishly swam. And swam. He kept swimming for what seemed like an eternity in a nautical hell.

Through fog so thick it was edible, Caleb finally spotted the ladder that led up to the commercial fishing-boat dock. He reached the ladder and latched on, then remained dizzily still for a few minutes.

He finally began to pull himself up each rung, one by one, as if they were the steps to Heaven's gate. Once he reached the dock, he was overcome by a violent seizure which left his tongue mangled, and then immediately he fell into unconsciousness.

Thanks to the kindness of a semi-geriatric lobsterman who was whiffing a nicely packed pipe full of Captain Black, Caleb eventually felt the gentle hand of a wild-haired Irish nurse checking for a fever in the Emergency Room at Gloucester's famous Addison Gilbert Hospital where, over the decades, so many fishermen had been generously treated for injuries sustained not only at sea but also in the gin-holes of one of New England's most notorious ports of call.

Caleb then flipped his thoughts as though they were an omelet in a Sunday morning frying pan, and he returned to the present. While he tried to warm himself, he pondered the dicey situation in which he now found himself.

He was a proud captain. He had never aspired to be a drug smuggler, and he cringed at the thought that he'd lowered himself to this, incessantly beating himself up for it. But what could he do? With all of the new government regulations and restrictions thrust upon the fishing industry, he and many of his colleagues saw "muling" as the only financial lifeline they could grab onto.

Tread water or drown . . .

Caleb's only solace was that, for once, the diesel engine wasn't bitching. He listened closely to gauge the rpm's. For the moment at least, the vessel was purring right along, and he allowed his right hand to lean a tad forward on the throttle in order to cordially invite a little more fuel to the dance.

Earlier That Day: Onion, Deckhand

Just as Onion shoved three warm Budweisers into a paper bag, he heard First Mate Sputnik yell, "We's leaving in ten minutes—gotta pick up the charter in twenty!"

Onion ran into the public restroom and almost crashed into some lavender-shirted daint from Hamilton who looked like a grandfathered-in, fourth-generation Myopia Hunt Club member.

Onion knew that heading out for the day with Captain Caleb meant four- to six-foot seas and the most rancid, flaccid bait that nickels could buy. Caleb's MO was to charge the charter clients the maximum amount allowed by common sense, and then get them so seasick offshore that they begged to come home and kiss the dock.

The result: collecting currency for a six-hour charter that lasted only a third of that time.

Extremely fuel-efficient was Onion's frequent thought. Nine out of ten paying parties (especially the corporate-outing guys who would play Mighty Joe Young and beat their chests before leaving port, only to be reduced to puddles of spittle halfway out) would be so embarrassed that they would never dare expose their lack of manhood by questioning either the price or the (laughable) potential for a refund.

What a noble way to do business and share the bounties of the sea, thought Onion.

Plus, First Mate Sputnik always had Onion swab the deck clean of the remnants of the passengers' lunch and pride, which was quite reminiscent of the famous *Helen H* trips from Hyannis Harbor out into the Gulf Stream. This thought, as always, led to his bitter, resentful reflections on the new fishing restrictions: *Friggin' government bow-ties didn't even have the courtesy to offer us a decent reach-around . . . tax dollars at work . . . what a farce . . .*

As Onion threw the toilet seat down and proceeded to feign a bathroom break, he inhaled the aforementioned cans of beer in hopes that this would provide fortification for at least the amount of time that it would take for the first paying passenger to turn the color of a Galapagos iguana. So often, it was the guy with the most expensive reel, the new Orvis outerwear, and the highest credit limit on his Amex Black . . .

Chapter 10

Trav and McGill

With only the slightest slur to his voice, Trav admitted, "So we have this client at the firm who's account has grown way too fast over the years, given his mundane occupation."

McGill was half listening to Trav, and half fixating on the waitress's thong-shot that was Ali/Frazier-smacking his gaze away from the co-ed attempting to bury the five-ball in the corner pocket of the billiard table ten feet away.

Unaware that he had less than McGill's full attention, Trav went on, "So this guy ended up on the kind side of some land deal a few years back, with every intention of developing the typical dream-site that they all build today—you know, mixed use. He wanted condos, office space, retail, as well as a big ol' anchor spot to tuck in something creative like a Target or a Best Buy.

"The long-time waterfront neighbors got all hot about it, but there wasn't much they could do, 'cause he spooned out just the right amount of three-bear porridge to the local city council and the conservation commission. So he's got this amazing piece of real estate with lease options and development-rights proposals all over the East Coast, but he's just been sitting tight.

"My contact at City Hall tells me that his tax checks clear, and Miss Jiggle-Tits down at the bank swears that he's current with the debt service. He's got the green light to stick a shovel in the ground, but to everyone's surprise he just keeps letting the underbrush grow thicker—more and more of an eyesore, you know?

"Well, the neighbors who initially were wringing their hands over his ultimate plans for the land, now dream of the day when they'll wake up to neon lights and Volvo wagons, versus the wasteland that this guy has let the plot evolve into.

"So . . . the worst of it is that this scoundrel has been cashing in on the tax credits he's getting from both the city and the state, and yet he still hasn't kept up his end of the bargain to develop the land for the 'common good'—whatever that farce of a term means.

"Now he's got the attention of the D.A.'s office and some heat is starting to come down—a complete drag for me, since his account was starting to beef up, and he doesn't complain when the friggin' Nasdaq tanks for a month or so. Dream client. Quiet phone. You know the type—no trade too small, no commission too big . . .

"Apparently, they got some hoity-toity upstart young broad attorney named Marlene Dunn on the case, who is hell-bent on not leaving a piece of meat on any of the bones she attacks.

"Not sure where she went to school, but sounds like a typical B.U. bitch to me . . ."

Chapter 11

Marlene

Marlene Dunn leaned into her car horn as if she were pushing a shopping cart full of cinder blocks up black diamond trail at Killington.

"C'mon! Move your ass!" she hollered against the relentless metronome-like taunting of her wiper blades.

Traffic annoyed Marlene. And when it was coupled with rain, she was tempted to just drive the damned Lexus over the edge of Tobin Bridge into the Mystic River, while feeling every emotion except regret.

Marlene never felt regret.

The beautiful young district attorney had much to be worried about, for she was due at a hearing across town in twenty minutes and the vehicles surrounding her were driving like they were on route to Perdition.

With a flash of her hands, Marlene ripped the wheel hard to the port side in order to try to pass the moonbat Prius in front of her.

She may have looked more like a runway model than a Nascar driver—kind of a Danica Patrick meets *Blue Blood*'s Bridget Moynihan, but her aggressive driving had become the stuff of legend around the courthouse.

She brought that same level of intensity into the courtroom, and oftentimes juries were left in shock at how this bombshell could crush the arguments of some of the best defense teams in Boston. Her sky-high cheekbones and downy lips tended to relax the opposition, who, without fail, would let down their guard and thus give Marlene the opportunity to slice the oratorical jugular. The ghosts of so many bloated, well-seasoned Boston defense lawyers lay strewn about the courthouse stairs that you could still catch a whiff of lunchtime Cutty Sark snifters and wannabe Cuban cigars.

At a very early age, Marlene had learned that being born physically attractive had its advantages—for that was the only advantage she was born with. And growing up in a household full of boys (if their shabby, crowded home could have qualified as a "household" according to the Commonwealth's census bureau), Marlene also learned at a very young age to fight for what she wanted. Her five brothers gave her neither any slack nor any old-school, British Navy–type quarter. Even with two of her siblings residing comfortably at St. Michael's Cemetery, and one in prison for at least another two years, Marlene wore an unabashed pride in herself, along with a chip on her shoulder the size of Spectacle Island.

Simmering with thoughts of frustration and anger at everyone and everything, she selected her next adversary, which at the moment appeared to be Boston's infamous gridlocked traffic.

Marlene suddenly thought of her brother Micky.

Micky Dunn was a man of few words. That's because Micky Dunn had been relieved of his heavy skull by a two-bit, one-shit, walking dildo behind a South Boston bar because of a nonsense football bet.

Everyone blames or embraces the snow when it comes to late-season NFL point spreads. Anyway, it was after a heated discussion of this very subject that Micky took the famous-player-signature end of a baseball bat.

And the reason that he became so quiet was that he subsequently came to reside at St. Michael's.

Not in the rectory . . .

However, he will stay quietly simmering in green grass and worm-ridden soil.

Marlene thought back to when they were kids. She so looked up to Micky, and he was worth looking up to. Sure, he was plenty rough-and-tumble, but not at all a bad guy—a couple too many pints, a couple too many football cards, and a few too many loose words.

Micky always had a close connection with Marlene, and he treated her not so much as a revered kid sister but rather as a princess. He knew damn well the obstacles that were ahead of her and what her environment had created as a horizon. As a big brother it broke his heart, and he tried to teach her that there was indeed a world out there, beyond that horizon, where she could thrive, and she could own it if she chose.

On Saturday mornings, Micky had a standing meeting at the gym with some of the neighborhood guys. He would always bring Marlene, not just in order to keep an eye on her, but more importantly to show her that there was more to life than the day-to-day neighborhood.

Marlene was always excited to go along. She loved to swim. Swimming was so important to her because once she was in the pool her body was free and, at least for that day, the water doused the hot-pavement thoughts that burned her aspirations.

She swam. And swam.

Micky would go off and always leave Marl with a pair of sawbucks and remind her where she could buy a grilled cheese and a Coke, and maybe take a shot at a few video games.

Marl used to sift through her brother's bag during their rides to the gym. She wasn't nosy—just curious. She would often find an empty bottle of some kind of whiskey or "something" buried within the tired, worn-out leather of Micky's gym bag. A little sadly, Marlene realized that this seemed to be a family tradition passed down from their father.

So many lessons are hard to unlearn . . .

Actually, though, she wasn't really all that concerned, for at that point in her life she believed that this was just what people did. Normal . . .

One day at the gym, she did not feel like running around the track, and did not feel like playing yet another lonely game of Asteroids. Since it was winter, and she was chilled to the bone, she decided to head for the pool area for a long, relaxing soak in the hot tub.

Normally, sat the gym , but today she felt fortunate to encounter a nice man who, while quite older, seemed like he would be interesting to talk to.

Marlene got into the hot tub to warm her cold body. Even at a young age, she was well aware of the hardships of a long New England winter.

The gentleman spoke, asking her about her school.

Marlene, unaware that there were actually predators among us, innocently shared a great deal of information about her life.

He mentioned Marlene's bathing suit. How pretty it was. That perfect lavender hue.

"May I touch it?" he asked.

Marlene, ever the pleaser, immediately complied.

It was only when Marlene felt a probing knuckle rubbing hard against her clitoris that she knew this was not normal . . .

Chapter 12

Captain Caleb Frost and Onion

"Hey, Caleb—you hear sumthin' about that m-m-mora . . . mora-tori . . . ? Whatever! You know what I mean!"

"No more catchin' friggin' cawd. And da thing is being 'stended for another s-s-season?"

asked a deeply frustrated Onion, who often stuttered when talking to Captain Caleb because any kind of authority tended to make him nervous. In fact, the poor bastard had a stutter as long as an old-school Ron Jeremy money shot.

Poor Onion.

He had been born with a condition that rendered his facial skin several shades of pink and yellow. The doctors were befuddled.

Hence his moniker . . .

Caleb was always fascinated to discuss maritime topics with Onion, for even though his deckhand was as dumb as a bag of nickels, at the same time he was a sweet man and a loyal friend, and very much on top of anything that would affect their livelihood. Onion couldn't tell you what he had for breakfast, or which Shakespeare character recited the Queen Mab speech, but he sure as hell knew when some government vegan ponytail was queering the place where his bread was being buttered.

Onion was born for the cold North Atlantic, and everyone knew that he would most likely die there, too. It was rumored that he had a mistress and a kid in every major port from Cape Elizabeth to Cape Hatteras. It was also whispered that if you gathered all of his "wives" together in a single dental office, you *maybe* could string together one full set of communal teeth. Even if most of these stories weren't entirely true, it *was* true that his moral fabric was . . . weak, and under the pressure of his perfectly honorable intention to provide at least something for these various women and children, he would try pretty much anything to turn a buck.

To Onion's question about the moratorium on cod fishing being extended yet again, Caleb replied, "Yeah, man, looks like another long, cold winter—"

Onion interrupted, "Y-y-y-yeah, and the sons of b-bitches are sayin' that the fisherman are turning to running smack, so's to not only make ends meet, but to also stick a finger in the air to the greenies in the government. Imagine us, Cap, dinkin' around with that brown s-s-shit?"

Caleb looked away across Gloucester Harbor, past the workaday bustle of fishing trawlers and lobster boats.

"Cap," Onion continued with fervor, "I ain't gonna get caught doing that and have to spend another five long years in the think tank just because I can't pay my bills—never could pay them anyway—fuck it . . ."

Onion stared at Captain Caleb in a rare moment of intense clarity.

Caleb did not protest. He embraced his role in life as a failure, and accepted that he would never be able to fire on all of society's mandated cylinders. His ex-wife made sure to cement that sentiment in his brain like a cinder block.

The object of his obsession was named Leslie, and for years the stark vision of her beauty had burned like an iron brand, scarring his every memory—waking moments and fitful dreams alike. It was always the tempestuous dreams that hurt the most, for they were the most unforgiving, the most relentlessly vivid, leaving their dark tracks across any fleeting peace.

Caleb paused. Even now, as they were readying the boat for a trip out to sea, his mind wandered a thousand miles away to where the vision of her face still left its faint vapor trail, like a ghost . . .

Caleb caught himself and returned to the topic at hand. "Yeah, Onion," he said. "Imagine us . . ."

The captain could process a thousand thoughts per second. He knew perfectly well that even if those around him constantly wrote him off as a dim-witted salty dog, he could easily get an acceptance letter from Harvard tomorrow.

Caleb walked down the gangway with short intermittent steps as he checked the lines that held the *Coney Island Whitefish* fast to the dock. He walked in this George Washington fashion, not because he was awkward or still feeling the last four days of eight-foot rollers, but more specifically because his mind was so painfully heavy with thought that he feared the weight of the day was making him top-heavy enough to fall into the chilly harbor.

He would not want that embarrassment. He would only welcome and encourage such a misadventure if jetty blocks were fastened to his fishing boots, once white but now stained red with the blood of thousands of fish.

It had been several years now since Caleb had run out of money while trying to make it in the real world, and the love of his life had run out of patience. Leslie had eventually boarded a plane back to the Alabama coast to live with her parents, and in the process she shattered his world by taking with her their three-year-old daughter, Avaline.

Like most men who take to the sea, Caleb feared the impending emptiness that came with every single night. At first, he was sleepless. Then came the nightmares.

In so many ways, he could not fault Leslie for relieving herself of such a disappointing life partner. She had to do what was best for her, he reasoned ruefully. As his world began to crumble, both personally and professionally, Caleb had turned to alcohol as his panacea of choice. His drinking soon evolved from a simple "taking the edge off" to a full-blown regimen that mixed in prescription drugs, which were all too conveniently available on so many North Shore wharves.

As a result, his body slowly began its conscientious objection, and quietly embarked upon a full physical shutdown. One of Caleb's less-than-proud moments came one morning when he began to shake to the point where it was impossible to pick up a spoon to eat his break-fast cereal. Within minutes, he was overcome by a full-blown alco-hol-and-benzo-withdrawal seizure—which, of course, was witnessed by Avaline, who gazed upon him with the most profound look of fear and terror, the faint look of love proving ancillary.

For injecting a speedball of horror into the veins of all those who witness such a physical tempest, a Stephen King tale has nothing on an alcoholic experiencing withdrawal . . .

As Caleb remembered the whole medical emergency, he was feeling confused before he blacked out completely, only to find himself in the ER at Addison Gilbert Hospital, where he was plugged into IVs and machines that beeped various unnerving tones.

That was a mind-crushingly frightful event for Avaline, and one that, unfortunately for him, would remain a tattooed image in her nightmares.

And the most unnerving part of the whole episode was that it was only the first of three . . .

No, he could not really blame Leslie for what Mark Twain called "light out for the territory," taking their cherished daughter in order to save the child from painful visions of her father's personal implo-sion—past, present, and future. Caleb had to admit that, in trying to survive, he had committed some horrible sins.

Now, he was just trying to make enough of himself that he could at least send some weak semblance of support to his wife and daughter, who were a world away. In his mind, they might as well have been on the moon. What did it matter, for he was far away in Hell.

The torment gnawed at him like a hunger that could never be sat-isfied, a thirst that could never be slaked. Meanwhile, he committed mental and emotional self-mutilation and chipped away at his being—less of him meant less that would hurt.

One day he woke up and discovered that the freezer was empty. And in some twisted way, that made it all so much easier—in fact, downright emancipating. Finally, but not surprisingly, the curtain was lifting to reveal that he had no soul, and it was time to make a deal with the devil. The thought appeared with an unfamiliar clarity that gave him a strange, warm feeling of comfort.

It was no secret to modern-day New England mariners that, what with technology-driven over-fishing coupled with liberal government intervention, the local fishing industry was in dire straits. It could not be claimed to be in a recession *per se*, for a recession inherently implies that it *will* indeed end someday. Captain Caleb Frost was not so certain that this cycle would ever truly turn.

Living and working in old seaport towns allowed Caleb a fine menu of characters with which to make acquaintance. One especially off-kilter fellow always struck him as rather interesting.

His name was Darby McBride. Darby hailed from Boston, and he spent his time in Gloucester not to book passage on a whale-watching expedition, but rather to sniff around the docks for something other than fresh bails of herring bait.

McBride was rumored to having been a distant business associate to the world-infamous Whitey Bulger and his Winter Hill cronies. McBride was supposedly on the hunt for fast vessels, and more importantly, captains who were seeking quick, albeit dangerous, infusions of cash.

When Darby first approached Caleb, he seemed just like any other unassuming tourist perusing the docks on a mild summer evening. He walked among the seemingly endless rows of vessels, unaware of the stark reality that thirty years earlier there had been three times as many boats berthed here.

"Hey there, Captain," he called out from the dock. "My name's Darby McBride. Up from Boston. I was just admiring your rig there and was wondering if you put her out for charter from time to time."

Caleb looked wary, but listened intently.

Darb continued, "You see, my colleagues and I have some cargo coming in from the north, and we're not quite sure that their boat carries enough fuel to make it all the way to Gloucester, if you understand my meaning? It would be mighty helpful if someone like yourself, well paid of course, were to head out there and greet my boys with another vessel in which to render transportation for the duration of the trip."

Caleb knew damn well what this meant. His first impulse was to throw a sloppy, ripped-up herring at this Darby McBride, but stopped short because he smelled an opportunity. This might be the window that he had been so desperately wishing for.

Any seaman who hung around the harborside gin joints knew that the drug trade coming down from the Canadian Maritimes was growing exponentially, with no clear end in sight. The opportunities were endless, but they were reserved for only those seasoned captains who were willing to risk everything in order to engage in Satan's favorite coastal trade: the smuggling of narcotics. And today's special on the menu was served up spoon-seared and brown . . .

Just to snap himself out of his dark-edged daydream, he barked at Onion, "Take your goddamned stutter pills or enroll in speech therapy—you sound like Billy Bibbit!"

He immediately regretted saying that. It was uncharacteristic—just another indication of the stress he was under. Onion was not a bad guy and was, if anything, annoyingly loyal.

"Hey, Onion," he said more softly. "I'm sorry—I really am. I didn't mean that. A stutter isn't such a huge setback. You do your job extremely well, and the clients love your . . . twisted charm."

Onion looked at him with sad puppy eyes.

"Onny," Caleb went on, "there was this girl that I went to Gloucester High with. Pretty girl, but very quirky and she came from a rough background. Her old man was a real sea dog who loved his 'cups,' and her mom . . . well, let's just say that her mom wasn't home all that often and spent many an hour at the wharfside gin joints. Anyway, this poor girl—albeit quite attractive, with a natural, primal flair—had her quirks. One such idiosyncrasy was that during class, and I'm confident that she was hardly even conscious of it, she would incessantly pick her nose . . ."

Onion just stared, looking confused. He didn't know whether or not it was okay to laugh.

"Anyway," Caleb continued, "the principal called her parents and explained that it was a distraction in the classroom and would the parents please bring their daughter to the doctor to see what could be done. Well, of course there was no way they were going to let her be seen by anyone in the medical business, lest they notice the bruises on the poor girl's body, which of course would immediately and correctly be tied back to her parents.

"So, instead of seeking professional medical or psychological assistance, the parents decided that every time their little angel was caught picking her nose in class, they would use her dad's cigar cutter to remove the offending finger.

"After a few months, the poor girl was down to two thumbs and one pinky. It was horrendously painful and embarrassing. For some reason, the teachers didn't seem to mind and they didn't make any inquiries, for at least she stopped disturbing the classroom dynamic.

"The young girl found herself even more of an outcast than ever, and she only found solace in her weekend trips to Rye Beach to go surfing. She could shred a surfboard better than any female surfer in New England, and this was the one environment where she wasn't judged and she could feel at peace.

"With her appendage challenge, she was unable to drive, and as a result she'd hitchhike every Saturday morning from Route 133 in Gloucester until she found someone heading north on Route 1.

"In fact, she was the most proficient and prolific Route 1 hitcher that America's oldest highway had ever seen. For with her physical beauty and her dexterity with what was left of her fingers, she was always guaranteed a ride in minutes. With one hand she would extend her thumb in order to notify drivers that she indeed was seeking a lift, and with her other hand that consisted of a thumb and a pinky, she was quite adept at flashing a very attractive 'hang loose' gesture . . ."

Deckhand Onion just stared. His brain was processing this like a garbage disposal does silverware.

"Captain Caleb—that s-s-story t-t-true?" asked Onion.

"Of course not, you dolt," replied Caleb. "However, the moral of the yarn is: Forget your friggin' stutter and don't look at it as a handicap. Play the hand that you're dealt and do the best that you can. Any obstacle can be overcome."

Damn . . . , thought Onion. *Captain is certainly a wise man* . . .

In his own way, Onion pondered the concept of wisdom and reflected on that for a moment.

Caleb, meanwhile, thought he smelled something burning, like a blown sterndrive.

Onion's thoughts suddenly set a course straight for his childhood memories. He remembered returning home from school with notes from the teacher that were to be signed by his parents. The school correspondence notified Onion's folks that his stutter was a distraction in the classroom and that the teacher wondered if Onion was performing some of it on purpose in order to gain attention.

Onion's parents read the letter, and his mom's immediate reaction was to hug her son and to tell him that they would get the best treatment available from a top-notch speech therapist. Unfortunately, they had no insurance at the time and so his mom would have to wait for her husband to secure a job with some decent health-care benefits.

Onion's dad, on the other hand, opted for a different approach. More of a hard-line, hard-working, coastal New England way to look at things. Onion's dad stared at his son. He then stared at the letter from the school. Then he stared at Onion yet again.

The right hook came very fast and with amazing fervor. Onion's dad's fist caught him square in the jaw and immediately broke said bone to the point where having Addison Gilbert Hospital wire it up would only be step one of the pain Onion would have to endure for a long, long time.

"Fuckin' retard," his dad growled. "Freak with four skin tones. What kind of circus act are you? Can't even talk like a human being, and you're dumb as a picked-over rack of ribs. You disgust me."

Onion just looked blankly ahead—he was in shock. His eyes were dimmed headlights trying to find a piece of straight road and a welcoming rest area where he could pull over.

The pain in his jaw was indeed acute, and after a few minutes he begged his mother to take him to the hospital, for his jaw, self-esteem, and soul were all completely broken.

As Onion's thoughts returned to the present, he semi-violently shook his head as if to jettison the painful memories of his violent father. "Hey, C-C-Captain Caleb!" he said brightly. "Evah notice that there are twenty-seven books in the New Testament, and all of our saviors died at twenty-seven? Cobain, Hendrix, Jim Morrison . . . ," Onion trailed off in thought.

Man, this is gonna be one long friggin' day, Caleb thought to himself. Overall, though, he felt happy about his coaching session with Onion, and eventually his thoughts returned to the memory of Leslie's unequaled beauty, which brought him back to one late Autumn night prior to her departure . . .

As he pulled into the driveway of their quaint home, he was puzzled to see how tightly the curtains had been drawn, and how few lights were on downstairs.

Caleb opened the door and began to climb the stairs, while simultaneously calling out Leslie's name. Kind of a modern-day "Honey, I'm home . . ."

Unbeknownst to Caleb, Leslie had crawled into a cannon, scraped the flint, and fired herself down the tacky-carpeted hallway.

He heard almost nothing before his senses were overwhelmed by the punches and kicks that violated his tired body.

The kicks were the worst. Kicks always triggered the sharpest stings and created the most frightfully beautiful purplish mosaic of bruises . . .

Caleb collapsed on the floor and steadfastly refrained from exchanging reciprocal blows to the many he was receiving. Instead, he huddled in the fetal position in the corner of the floor while praying for the sun to rise and erase the prior evening's strangeness.

Chapter 13

Jus and Sorta/ Kinda Marlene

Jus stared as a smartly dressed, radiant morsel waited impatiently in line ahead of him to order coffee.

Jus was used to staring, but usually it was through a long-range rifle scope.

This was odd, for Jus rarely fixated on anyone or anything. To "fixate" meant that, very secretly, you yearned for connection. For a touch of sharing. An exploration of another life, another world that was counterintuitive to Jus, who was perpetually the center of his own existence, and thus king of all that he surveyed. It meant that Jus had to accept that there was something, someone other than himself— which of course was an inconceivable concept for him.

What jarred Jus was what lit the flame of attraction. It was not the usual. Or at least, not something that he could easily process.

In this case, it was not her primal femininity, though that was certainly present.

It was not her flawless air.

Not that oh-so-caressable body, which had certainly bought a ticket for a ride in Jus's mind.

It was her shoulders . . .

Shoulders?

It was that radiant confidence that completely threw Jus's train off the rails of rational thought.

She is ravishing, he told himself.

For the first time in his cloudy memory, he begged his brain to dig into his internal Dewey Decimal System and research the last time that this particular type of book was pulled off the shelf.

He didn't want to stare too long, for he feared that she would notice his optical advances.

But he couldn't help himself. He had been hiding in the tall grass for too long.

Yet, he had to find out who she was . . .

And in due time, unbeknownst to Jus, he would—unfortunately.

A taxi horn blared outside of the chichi coffee shop, and Jus snapped back into "reality"—if indeed there was such a stop on the train route that circled through his private hell.

It was a brief feeling, yet so exhilarating. That powerful, yet short-lived rush like a nitrous oxide blast in the parking lot at a Phish show.

Can that feeling ever actually endure? Jus inquired of himself.

No . . . no, it cannot. Fortunately, foolish thoughts evaporated quickly for Jus, for he knew far too intimately that his heart was made of stone.

One quick head shake like a soaking-wet dog attempting to dry itself, and then without further hesitation he returned to business.

Jus hated fancy coffee. As a typical cynical Boston Irishman, he didn't give a rat's ass about the difference between a venti and a grande. He yearned to arrive at the counter, look the smug, trust-fund snot-dripper behind the counter in the eye, and say in his thickest, loudest, 3:00 A.M.—buzz of a Boston accent, "Give me a lahge reglah.

"With two sugahs.

"And a wicked lottah creeem . . .

". . . You fuckah!"

It was strange how at random moments Jus would slip into a doppelgänger role without the slightest bit of warning.

Appropriate, he would say to himself.

This, all while donning the finest that Brooks Brothers had to offer, and faintly smelling of thousand-dollar-an-ounce cologne and a lingering hint of stoic gun powder . . .

Jus sported quite the myriad of influences and contradictions.

Chapter 14

Captain Caleb Frost

Caleb violated his own rule whenever he peered into his journal so late at night. The journal was a pool of still water. He dropped a stone, and an echo would often retort with its lack of encouragement.

Sometimes the echo would be engulfed in seemingly endless blackness, and then the stillness would inevitably return.

Other times, the response was more painful—a shrieking quiet.

Exhausted from cleaning the *Coney Island Whitefish*, Caleb would often collapse on the deck and stare up at the near-dusk sky, and would tearfully beg the taunting clouds to let him share in the innocent dance that was his daughter's life.

He pleaded to some savior to reintroduce him.

He would beg with memory. Beg with visions and hopes. But most of all he would beg with the sting of harsh realities and soft song endings.

The tired eyes of the relatively young skipper (young in age, anyway) would peer out at the water that long ago had showered him with gifts of endless bounty, beauty, and possibility.

In time, that deep blue lost the battle to the now victorious, soulless, godless, vast gray expanse.

As the keys to the world's wonder chest were slowly being handed over to the endless black of night, Caleb reminisced about a piece of advice that a crusty old salt had once shared with him years ago: "Don't fool yourself and dance at dusk . . ." Caleb stared and the old seaman added, "In case dusk is really just that. Dusk . . ."

Caleb viewed the approaching night as the worthiest of adversaries. Kind of like a power hitter facing an ace pitcher with a perfect ERA— if Caleb gave a shit about baseball.

Now the blue of those perfect near-dusk moments marched among the ranks of the growing numbers of gray-colored uniforms.

Shaving had become a chore.

Every memory a tightening shackle.

He shuddered at taking showers, for he knew there was no way to truly cleanse himself. *Rime of the Ancient Mariner, my ass* . . .

Marlene

As Marlene patiently and rather dramatically paced the courtroom, she never took her glaring eyes off of the defendant who sat in the rickety wooden chair like a squirrel about to be run over by a Mack truck.

"Ladies and gentlemen of the jury," she began. "What you've heard today is a compelling argument. Hats off to the defense counsel, for they have formulated and downright fabricated quite the compelling scenario."

In response to that comment, the corpulent defense attorney merely shifted his fat ass in his chair.

Marlene continued, "The defense wants you to believe that the defendant, Mr. Simmons, acted in self-defense when he brutally stabbed his ex-wife—nineteen times. Yes, we all agree that the estranged couple were in the midst of an argument and subsequent altercation when the event took place. However, what my counterpart has failed to account for is, if said couple was indeed divorced and barely on speaking terms, then why is it that Mr. Simmons had multiple scratch marks on *all* parts of his body, and why was his semen was found on the victim's body?

"It appears to me, as it will to anyone hearing the past two week's testimonies, that there was a little bit more to Mr. Simmons' casual visit to Mrs. Simmons than was considered by the defense."

The defense attorney struggled to raise his massive belly out of his seat. "Objection, your honor!" he cried. "Complete speculation and misleading the jury!"

To which the judge responded, "Overruled. Please continue, Counselor Dunn."

Marlene did not skip a beat, despite the pain in her hand, which had lingered for all these years since her self-inflicted gunshot accident and which, without fail, would flare up during periods of extreme stress. "So let's perhaps agree that there indeed was another motive to Mr. Simmons' stopping by his ex-wife's house that evening. Perhaps a motive of a sexual nature born of lust, violence, and a need to control.

"Not to mention the fact that, statistically, a self-defense crime involves one, maybe two, stab wounds for the individual defending him- or herself, as they are usually in such shock that to continue the violence is not within their ability, either physically or emotionally. But Mr. Simmons stabbed his wife nineteen times!"

Marlene noticed out of the corner of her eye several of the jurors slowly nodding their heads.

"So I ask the members of the jury," she continued, "to place their decision in the hands of common sense and sound reasoning. This was not an act of self-defense, but rather a cruel act of brutal violence brought on by primal jealousy and pure inhuman rage.

"The prosecution rests, your honor."

Which was met by, "As does the defense . . ."

And with that, Marlene knew that she had drawn blood.

While the jury convened, Marlene left the courtroom and walked out into the lobby to clear her head and calm her nerves. These were the moments that drove her ambitions and made her feel alive. She had the utmost confidence that she had made the best argument possible, but after all, this was the People's Republic of Massachusetts, where both juries and judges tended to lean quite liberal.

"Counselor," said the bloated defense attorney as he approached Marlene from across the hall. "You did a mighty fine job in there. Hopefully, you don't actually believe that you're going to convict my client. There's not a spark lit in hell that's going to sway these twelve suckers to send this poor prick to Walpole. They're scared chickenshit and don't have the stones to do it. I'll bet you two martinis and a roll in the hay with yours truly that I'm correct."

Marlene almost vomited—partly because of what she just heard, and partly because of the reeking stench of Seagram's Seven that was wafting from her adversary.

"Counselor," she shot back, "your client is a filthy murderer who deserves to rot in the loneliest corner of Hell for what he did. He is a slithering Gila monster—much like yourself. And for the record, I could have the judge hold you in contempt if you were to take a breathalyzer test right now. See you back in court."

As Marl turned and walked away, she felt her ass get hot, for the obese defense council was staring at it with laser beams.

It took the jury less than an hour to deliberate, and all parties were called back into the courtroom.

Marlene sat patiently and noticed the look of confidence on the defense team across from her, as well as the look of sheer terror on the part of the defendant.

Finally, the lead juror stood. "Your honor," she said, "we members of the jury have come to a decision. We the jury find the defendant, Mr. Aaron Simmons, guilty on all counts."

With that the judge's gavel fell and Marlene glared at the defense attorney with a cobra's stare . . .

Jus and Marlene

A serpent's keen eye was a physical attribute second only to the callous, shrunken heart of a prolific assassin.

To say that Jus followed Marlene out onto the sidewalk would have been a laughable understatement. For he never followed anyone—he stalked. Jus would set a heat-seeking tracker onto his target, and his mind and body would sit back and let cruise control drive the hearse.

Fortunately for Marlene, Jus's interest in her was not "work-related." He kept to a respectable distance behind Marl and just watched her black shirt dance in the wind. He thought she was quite fortunate that her outfit was not doused in kerosene, for the heat generated by all of the male stares as she passed by would have certainly triggered spontaneous combustion.

Jus had to approach her. It was not a question of if, but when. As luck usually does with Justin, it found its way onto his craps table.

As Justin homed in on his target, he noticed a small slip of paper fall out of her briefcase. Here was his chance.

Jus reached down and picked up Marl's parking lot stub and quickly approached the beautiful assistant DA.

"Excuse me," he said cordially when he'd caught up to her. Jus knew that you never said, "Excuse me, miss," to a woman like Marlene Dunn, who radiated such self-confidence.

Marl turned quickly with a siren's eye.

Just as quickly, Jus attempted to diffuse her. "Counselor, it seems that you dropped something . . ."

Marl just stared and within a nanosecond took in Jus's aura. "Why, thank you, sir. You saved me from having to prove to the parking lot attendant that I had not been squatting in his lot since Flag Day. I'm curious—how did you guess my profession?"

Jus replied, "Well, some would say that I have a rather perceptive eye. Plus, you ordered your coffee back there like you were in the midst of a cross-examination . . ."

Marl pursed her soft lips. "Hmm. . . I didn't realize that it was that obvious."

And with that, Marl offered the closest thing to a flirty smile that had graced her high-cheek-bone visage in quite some time.

Jus smelled blood in the water. Not his fault. Nor is it ever the fault of a great white shark to sever the femoral artery of an unsuspecting surfer waiting for the next large swell. That was just how Mother Nature designed each respective predator.

"My name is Jus. I work nearby, and if you are indeed an attorney, my guess is that you could swing a cat and hit your office from here."

"I'm with the DA's office," Marl replied and extended her hand, almost as if she were already inviting him into her downy bed and soft, cool silk sheets. "I can tell already, by your swagger and attire, that you most likely play for the dark side. Big firm, I surmise . . ."

Jus was flattered. "Yeah, the public is often quite confused about who are the good guys and who are the bad guys in my world. For me, it's quite simple. I'm just a hired gun."

Pun intended.

"I enjoy your banter," Jus continued. "Any chance that maybe you'd care to join me for a glass of wine at the Sail Loft after work next week? It would be interesting to get to know you."

Marl replied, "Wow. . . The Sail Loft. . . Big spender. . . Tough times at the firm?" she added with a dirty wink.

Jus was hooked. "Actually," he replied, "I just like to keep things simple. And efficient . . ."

And with that, Marlene Dunn shared with Justin the one secret that she kept locked away even more tightly than her inner thoughts: her cellphone number.

Marlene

Sundays were always the toughest day of the week for Marlene Dunn.

While the world around her rested and sought peace, Sunday was when her insanely focused and intellectual mind would scream and thrash her with whips of vengeance for what she had had to endure during the prior six days.

A lover was out of the question. Her demeanor would have made Camelot's walls look like they were made of papier mâché.

As Marlene adjusted her headphones and tightened the laces of her two-hundred-dollar running shoes, she caught the eye of an overweight, middle-aged cigar smoker staring at her breasts like they were a winning Powerball ticket.

To Marlene, that was just a routine annoyance. She had been used to the attention and affection of the male population since she first shed her training bra, and the malicious glances she shot back in return had not softened with age.

One benefit for Marlene of having so much testosterone oozing through her house while she was growing up was that she did not necessarily need to learn the hard way that men were inherently mud-covered pigs. She had eavesdropped on her brothers enough times as they compared war stories on a Sunday morning during the NFL pregame to understand that even when you peeled away the ridiculous embellishments and overstatements, men were certainly the age-old enemy.

Subhuman remoras, thought Marlene.

Today's run was to be relatively short due to the humidity already rising despite the early hour. To justify such a quick three-mile course, Marl committed herself to a seven-minute-mile pace.

As she set out, her mind immediately shut off the outside world and her thoughts began to rise like a cobra out of a Mumbai basket. This new case to which she was assigned was definitely out of her comfort zone.

Not only did Marlene not like technology, but she still had nothing but contempt toward her fellow classmates, wallowing in their pathetic geekdom. Every once in a while, some pencil-gnawing nerd's algorithm would indicate that it was time to venture out of his comfort zone ask Marlene out for coffee.

To which she would reply, "I don't drink coffee, you tool! But obviously you do, 'cause your breath smells like dog-ass!"

Ahh . . . ever the sweet, delicate dandelion, as she was widely known . . .

In the midst of this rare moment when she force-fed a Jimi Hendrix dose of Ativan to her cell phone, Marlene was beginning to fret about this new case in which she was going to have to conduct an investigation and subsequently try to prosecute, for she had zero experience with technology firms and absolutely no history or knowledge of infractions within the financial or securities world.

As a rabid Pearl Jam fan, Marlene thought that SEC stood for, "Shit, Eddie's Cute . . ."

BeamTech was the name of the tech firm whose shares had gone public, and Shea & Rizzo Securities had distributed the limited offering. The district attorney stuck Marl with the case—mostly, she thought, because she had consistently declined his advances at each of the last five office Christmas parties. She rarely socialized outside of the office, and within the confines of the courthouse she was not exactly Donna Reed.

Marlene was trying to compile an initial overview of what the hell had gone wrong with S&R's selling of the shares. The brokerage firm had a reputation for being a dumping ground for brokers who had gotten frosted from more distinguished peer firms. Despite having a record of countless misdemeanor-type violations for their trading and business practices, S&R had thus far managed to evade the night-vision laser scope of the SEC as well as the other self-regulating entities such as FINRA.

This time, though, the chess board looked a little different.

As Marlene finished up mile one in just under eight minutes (*I'm dragging ass*, she accused herself), she could not help but to review the case notes in her mind and surmise that for some reason S&R had taken an unnecessarily huge risk with BeamTech, even by their standards.

Marl's thoughts meandered to that famous quote from *The Godfather*: "Tom, this is business and this man is taking it very personal . . ."

What she was trying to squeeze out of her thoughts was that there must have been some other compelling reason for S&R to find itself in such hot water with the powers that be. "Follow the money" is always the easiest directive when investigating a malfeasance case, but this one seemed to be even more complicated. Marlene figured that it must have something to do with money *and* sex, for in her mind that was pretty much all people were interested in anyway.

Marlene rarely gave to charity.

When asked to donate a dollar at the Walgreens checkout, Marl merely stared at the underpaid cashier. To utter the word *no* would have been downright gratuitous.

Marlene's sourness would sometimes force her thoughts to teenage memories of *The Sandman* . . .

When Marl was young, still swimming in the whirlpool of youth that wanted to drown her, she could still conjure up hopes of an eventual silver lining.

She sniffed the air. She sniffed and caught a scent that told her that things could get better. There could be a way out . . .

Marl's mom, upon realizing that her daughter might actually go to the prom, decided to buy her a dress. A shamelessly beaming red dress. Blue did not match her overall look, and green would never be appropriate for a girl like Marlene. There were not a lot of dresses gracing the hangers in Marlene's childhood home.

Her date was not a bad guy. Typical awkward idiot in the presence of a girl gone woman who was polished up with primal and sensual beauty.

Keeps the species going.

The prom was wonderful. Yes, nausea was prevalent due to the band's seventies-riddled song list, but 'twas the proverbial good time had by all.

The limo pulled up to the beach, and the cheesy, slick-haired ponytail limo driver opened the doors with all the pomp of a drop-off at the Oscar red carpet. He would have looked perfect on the front of a Beefeater gin bottle.

So fun are the friends. Champagne and laughs. The future was screaming off of life's dashboard like a Sunday-morning blaze.

Marl's date helped her out of the limousine. He held her left hand while clutching her wine glass in his right.

She looked nothing short of ravishing!

All of the self-esteem that had been drained away. . . All of the verbal and emotional pain that had been jettisoned . . .

They walked the beach, and then fell onto the soft sand while proceeding to quickly undress one another.

As said idiot rolled around and strained to don the condom, he forgot one basic aspect of having sex on the beach: a condom is all-welcoming to its surroundings.

Dumb-ass got sand all over it!

And proceeded to be the moment's Romeo!

"*Owww!*" screamed Marlene. "That friggin' hurts, you troll!"

And there went Marl's dream of a Cinderella prom, as well as any chance that she would extend her grace to another male member of the human race.

For Marl was not the only victim whose soul took lashings in the back. Every string to which she ever reverberated in the future would feel the dampness . . .

Marl felt a lot of *owww*'s in her life.

The worst was when one of her brothers (who doted on her—not bad guys, just bulls in the china shop of life) gently tossed a gun to her and said with a desperate calm, "Please hide this, pumpkin . . ."

Unfortunately, that bullishness was an inadvertent gift from her dad. It seemed that her dad and brothers were involved in some kind of "making things right" issue when the plasterer down the street began making advances on Marl's cousin. Apparently, the plasterer had taken a liking to the young girl, yet the feelings were not exactly reciprocated.

One of Marl's brothers, who was already due in superior court and felt that he had nothing to lose, decided that retribution might be in order and invited the plasterer to Foley's for a drink.

Quick drink, as was the take-away for Marl's brother's friends, for the plasterer ended up in the would-be *Wicked Tuna* end of the transom of the boat.

Long day.

Marl could only imagine what events had led up to her receiving said gun.

She spoke to her girlfriend that night.

The gun really jarred her.

Yet. Intrigued her.

She spoke into the phone and slowly described to her girlfriend her feelings while holding the gun.

She spun the revolver around while the thoughts danced in her head as if they were being paid by Barnum & Bailey . . .

POW!

Marl was quiet. Marl was serene.

Things like this don't happen to Marl, for *she* is the smart one in the family.

Marl looked down as the blood seeped, not spilled, just seeped from the hole that she accidentally shot through her hand.

Initially, Marl was horrified. Her thoughts were to yell to her mother. Yell to her brothers. Yell to the world!

Yet in the end, she relaxed . . .

In the end it was peaceful . . .

In the end, she invited her cat to investigate and taste "life" . . .

Jester Chauncey and Marlene

Marlene entered the office park with a certain trepidation. To make a surprise call on a man like Jester Chauncey was tantamount to compromising her investigation into his business practices.

She entered the office's rather tacky waiting area and approached the bleach-blonde receptionist.

"Assistant District Attorney Marlene Dunn here to see Mr. Jester Chauncey."

To which the response was simply, "Ma'am, do you have an appointment?"

Marlene would rather have been called an asshole than "ma'am." That in itself was a subtle insult.

"Please let him know that I apologize for showing up unannounced," she said, mustering all the politeness at her command. "However, this concerns a very important matter. An *appointment* I don't have, but a *subpoena* I do . . ."

The receptionist stared for a moment with a jackal's glare.

"Let me see if he's available . . ."

Five minutes later, Marlene was briskly escorted down the long death-row-like hallway to the office of S&R's CEO, Jester Chauncey.

He rose from his chair behind the oversized anachronistic oak desk and politely extended his hand across his belt-challenging, scotch-and-sirloin-bloated stomach. "Pleasure to meet you, counselor," he said, gesturing toward a chair in front of the desk. "What brings you to visit our fine operation? Did you know that we have been serving the Greater Boston investing public since 1983, and that we maintain a very loyal book of clients throughout the region? Many of whom have relocated to second homes in Florida and the Caribbean by ways of profits from the accounts that we have diligently managed over time."

Seating herself and clasping her hands atop the briefcase she had positioned on her lap, Marlene responded, "Our office has thoroughly combed through your firm's history. Congratulations on your success. However, today I am here to discuss another matter."

At that, Jester suddenly became quiet and merely stared and listened.

"Mr. Chauncey," she began, "the district attorney has been receiving 'information' regarding a company known as BeamTech for whom you have been moving shares via your firm at quite the premium compared to fair market price, in our opinion.

"At this point, we are not calling it a 'pump and dump,' but we don't like the looks of several of your recent transactions. And to be a little more frank, while your firm has seen quite a bit of success under your impressive guidance, you have several compliance violations and broker/dealer inquiries that are still pending and under investigation.

"Bottom line—we don't think these transactions pass the smell test."

Jester leaned back in his chair, and all Marlene could do was wonder how said piece of furniture did not collapse under the sheer weight of his girth.

Jester smiled and cleared his throat. "Attorney Dunn. My firm maintains the highest level of ethical standards. It is kind of you to stop by today and inform me of this farce of an investigation. However, unless you have tangible and significant proof of any malfeasance, I would politely ask you to excuse yourself and let me get on with what has turned out to be quite the busy day.

"If you choose to remain on our premises, you are more than welcome here, and I shall have my assistant find you a comfortable work space. However, in the interim while you set up shop, I would like to request a little time to reach out to my attorney, for I don't appreciate being threatened and steamrolled within the confines of my own office."

By now his smile had faded, and he leveled a hard gaze at her. "You make the call, Ms. Dunn. Thank you for your time and concern for our investing public."

And with that, Marlene knew that this was going nowhere at the moment and that, with those comments, it was Jester who had drawn first blood.

Marlene vowed to herself that she would see this snake oil salesman in court . . .

Chapter 15

Home of S&R's CEO, Jester Chauncey

"Whaddya mean we have to sell the Palm Beach condo! Bullshit! Unacceptable!" screamed Jester's wife.

They had been married for eight years. She was twenty years his junior in age.

Mrs. Chauncey version 3.0 was quite a talented lass, for she could multitask with the best of them by berating her failing husband, picking out her poodle's socks for the day, and texting her trainer that, though she might be ten minutes late, she could promise him a handjob—and all while being feverishly careful not to damage the nails she'd had manicured the day before.

Jester did his faltering best to quell the steaming woman's demeanor. "Listen, honey," he pleaded. "It's only temporary. I have a *lot* of problems at the firm right now and I need to start raising some cash for what are certain to be exorbitant legal expenses, as well as try and sock a little something away in that safe in your mom's attic."

The safe was a handy hiding place for Jester to squirrel away anything that he did not want anyone (especially the woman glaring at him) to view. It worked out quite well, because Jester, and *only* Jester, had the combination, which was branded into this memory: 3122006. The date that he decided it was time for his secretary to work on her "shorthand."

And subsequently decided that it was finally time to have his second wife killed . . .

The beautiful and enraged love of Jester's life continued, "Why don't you be a *real* man and figure a way out of this disaster. Unless you've suddenly found Jesus, I seem to recall that you have quite a handy way of cleaning up your messes . . ."

Her comments did twist the wires in Jester's head a bit. Maybe there was a way to conjure up some quick cash so that the lawyers could keep the balls bouncing in the air with the SEC and IRS for a few years, which would be just long enough for Jester to concoct a proper scheme for faking his own death and making off with enough money to retire to the Caymans for a life of comfort and whores. His plan all along had been to snuff out the shrew standing before him, but that seemed too easy, too elementary.

Better to have some fun and introduce her to some horny bastard that he hated.

A few months back, Jester had just left an afternoon meeting when a sudden craving lured him to the line at Pizzeria Regina in Boston's Quincy Marketplace. It was well after lunchtime, but business was typically brisk at the famous purveyor of cheese slices.

Jester noticed that the guy in front of him looked like an older version of a good friend from Charlestown High School, a guy with whom he had lost touch over the years, as they selected decidedly different career paths.

"Darby? Darby McBride? Is that you?" asked Jester.

Normally, it was extremely dangerous to startle Darby McBride from behind. Odds were rather high of his spinning around to greet you with a right hand to shake, and a 9-millimeter in his left.

Darby immediately recognized his old friend. "Well, I'll be dipped in shit . . . Jester Chauncey . . . looking sharp. How long has it been? Hey, lemme grab you a slice and let's spend a few minutes catching up—if you have the time?"

Darby sensed from his old buddy's tailored suit and matching dental work that Jester had done all right for himself over the years. Darby smelled money. And such an aroma to Darby McBride was sweeter than twenty-year-old Scotch or the panting breath of the highest-grade Vegas call girl.

"That sounds great, Darb. I'll snag us a table . . ."

The two old friends sat and bantered for a few minutes over their steaming slices, but quickly their instincts kicked in that they might be of use to one another. This encounter could provide Darby with a potential investor in a new heroin run. He explained that he was collaborating with some poor down-on-his-luck fishing slob on the North Shore to transport some . . . "product."

Jester, sensing an opportunity to add a little something to his legal defense fund, nodded eagerly and said, "Hey, Darb. This opportunity on the North Shore sounds quite interesting and potentially quite profitable. Before we discuss how we might proceed, I'm just curious—"

Darby stopped him mid-sentence. "Whaddya, scared 'cause it involves selling drugs? Hey, man, get in the real world."

"Darb," said Jester, shaking his head. "Darb. Do not rush to conclusions. Do you know the difference between peddling narcotics and selling widows and orphans shares of some two-bit sham of a penny stock? Same difference as between a bitch and a cur."

They both laughed.

"No," Jester went on. "My inquiry involves some of your other, more . . . esoteric consulting services."

Darby pursed his lips and raised his eyebrows, inviting his old friend to continue.

"You see," Jester said, "I have this thorn in my side named Assistant District Attorney Marlene Dunn. She's making both my personal and professional lives quite arduous, you understand, and is really just taking up too much space in this city.

"Remember the old days, Darb? Remember when some poor soul would wake up and put on a pot of coffee, and maybe then put some food and water out for the dog? And then, casually walk out to the front of his quaint suburban home to snag his freshly delivered *Globe* and *Herald*, only he would never make it back to the kitchen?

"Yes, of course there would be scuttlebutt and the usual farce of an investigation, but that swarm of bees would quickly give way to normalcy."

Darby nodded, smiling slightly.

"The sun would still rise," Jester continued. "The tide would still ebb and flow. Both the roosters and the T subway cars would start screeching at the same time each morning.

"And the world would forget said newspaper subscriber. It would be as if he never existed . . ."

Darby remained uncharacteristically quiet for a few seconds. Then he looked his friend squarely in the eye and said, "Jester. The Angiulos are gone. Whitey is gone. We can't just go taking out judges and politicians like during the Golden Age. Nowadays you gotta worry about some ten-year-old filming your hit on a fuckin' phone and sending it to some fancy Internet thing in China. It's not the same. And nowadays, it certainly doesn't come cheap. Back then, we could hire some deadbeat gambler or coke addict to take somebody out for the price of an eight-ball of Columbian snow. Those days are over, my friend . . ."

Jester smiled sadly. "Yeah, Darb," he agreed. "Those days are over, but if it's one thing I learned in business, it's that you need to evolve with the times and adapt. And from what I hear, for a throwback who's hanging onto the glory days, you have a pretty good relationship with one of the new breed. Perhaps he doesn't come cheap, but neither does a hand job in Hong Kong anymore. . .

"Will you at least talk to him on my behalf? Think about it. I'll get you financing for your Gloucester project. You get a nice finder's fee for removing this DA thorn in my ass, and I pick up some scratch to keep the legal wolves at bay on my end so I can get my shit together and prepare for an untimely fake death and subsequent disappearance. Everyone's happy . . .

"Plus, you can't help loving the rush of putting a deal together, can you, ol' Darb?"

Darb had to admit it: he still loved the rush. Viagra had nothing on the surge that came from setting wheels in motion while holding the strings.

Marlene

The perfectly sculpted derriere of the young assistant district attorney fidgeted in the seat of her Lexus. This whole issue of BeamTech's connection to Shea & Rizzo was really gnawing at her most natural instincts. Marlene had a funny feeling that Jester Chauncey of Shea & Rizzo Securities was going to rue the day that he started pushing the envelope so far as to get her involved.

You see, Marlene had an innate craving for the truth—which is what she told herself, anyway. However, what really drove Marlene's soul to the pinnacle of cotton-sheet-ripping climax was the act of vanquishing an opponent . . .

From an early age, Marl realized that she was born with a killer instinct that could only be deepened by the events of her life and the people presented to her by the gray-eyed world.

You see, the people who seemed to find themselves within Marlene's steel-fibered fish net always, without fail, found trouble. Practicing law provided her with a natural gladiator pit in which to swing the sword and draw back the bowstring of vengeance upon the world.

She viewed an opportunity for victory like an eight-year-old staring at the chimney on Christmas Eve.

Graced not only with good looks but also a primal, radiant sexuality, she of course garnered the attention of many suitors who had no idea what chemicals they were playing with in the science lab of the brain that resided in the head of Marlene Dunn.

She once entered into a tryst with a charming, handsome, and successful heath care executive who seemed to possess a rare and powerful hold over Marlene, melting her usual coldness. They met in Columbus Park while each was engaging in a warm-down after a run during a particular humid New England summer afternoon along the public walkway that runs the perimeter of the south side of Boston Harbor. It was the type of urban green space that, even with only a few people around, seemed crowded on a Sunday afternoon in June. If you took away the Betty Warren–voting soccer moms and overprotective yuppie dog-owners, the place would resemble Atlantic City in 1982.

John Tessio was particularly dashing and inviting, with a smile that belonged in a Crest commercial. The two exchanged lightning glances, and within two hours they were swapping bodily fluids back at Marlene's rented North End rooftop condo.

To Marlene, such a casual sexual encounter was indeed rare, but she rose to the challenge of John's charisma and his primal, musk-like demeanor . . .

The two began dating and sharing every night together when John did not have to put in overtime at the St. Eligius Hospital, which was in the midst of a major renovation made possible by a generous donation from a wealthy Swiss international hedge-fund manager. He had med-flighted his wife from Zurich to Boston for a one-chance-in-a-million last-minute heart procedure that saved her life from a rare, degenerative cardio condition.

He was also rumored to be a card-carrying member of the Illuminati, like his great-great grandfather.

Anyway, when John was not fending off his CFO and Marlene was done picking the meat off the bones of prominent Boston defense attorneys, the two enjoyed quick getaways to such romantic destinations as Woodstock, Vermont, and the unique wine country of Long Island's North Fork. Certainly, due to the demands of their careers and the fact that they each were *so* damned important, they couldn't even entertain the thought of more than two nights away.

Finally, when some natural cord was struck within Marlene, she summoned up the courage to discuss the "future." "John," she began, "these last several weeks have been a dream for me. I just want to talk to you about the future, and if there is one for us. What are your honest feelings about us?"

Upon hearing Marl's opening argument, John Tessio became un-characteristically subdued, which both saddened and infuriated her.

This was one of the few times that she actually envisioned herself in the role of wife and mother, and John would be her prince, who had chased her on a white steed one Columbus Park afternoon.

John looked into Marlene's eyes and said, "Marl, I really need to contemplate such a dramatic change in lifestyle . . . but I'll be in touch."

Marl was immediately infuriated, but that sentiment gradually morphed into a sense of defeat—a very foreign feeling for her.

Purely out of curiosity, she began to investigate the background of one John Tessio. This was something that she would normally have done right at the outset of a relationship, for she had access via the court system to pretty much anything about a person save their favorite sex position.

Marlene uncovered that John Tessio was indeed John Tessio. The same John Tessio who had seven times been arrested and convicted for soliciting a prostitute.

Marl's jaw dropped.

It seemed that these were not high-priced, scrubbed-and-waxed professional call girls who always gave money to the local state-house hacks and who supported legalized gambling in Boston. Instead, they were rather common nickel whores with whom one may transact business behind an abandoned rail car next to a Blue Line subway station. They were affectionately referred to as "rail screechers."

Marlene was white-hot livid. But the real *crème de la crème* of John Tessio's biography was the fact that there also existed a Mrs. Tessio, and this was not John's mom.

True, John did not lie about his job. He was indeed the top dog at a major Boston hospital. However, said medical facility was not at all involved in a critical expansion project, for they were *far* too busy holding meetings with the US Attorney's office to discuss multiple counts of Medicare fraud, all of which had occurred during John's tenure. Pesky feds.

And yes, John did indeed spend countless hours with his CFO. However, this was to draft responses to the feds while simultaneously having his temperature checked via the prison way.

John's poor wife resided in the dark, but by all accounts she enjoyed her stay as long as the private-school tuition fees and the Brae Burn Country Club membership dues were current.

Marl was pissed! Pissed to the point where her bones surged the color of lemon-lime Gatorade . . .

See, the question at hand was not whether or not John would need to be taken behind the proverbial woodshed. No, the question was how, and a little Irish luck provided Marlene with the answer served on a silver platter. His name was Tommy McInnen.

Tommy was a stereotypical neighborhood Mick. Rap sheet a mile long, wrought with street-punk petty crimes since the late nineties. Marlene had convicted this guy so many times that whenever he entered the courtroom, she could tell how many days it had been since he shaved or downed his last slug of Jameson's.

Marl saw the opportunity as one of mutual benefit to both her and Tommy.

Excited as a trapped miner clawing his way out of a deep shaft, she entered the interrogation room with an uncharacteristically wide smile, or so thought Tom's state-appointed public defender.

Marl sat, and after exchanging extremely brief pleasantries, she leaned toward the detainee and said, "See, Tom. This time it's serious. How long have we known each other? Fifteen years, easy—right? Shit, I felt quite slighted that you didn't invite me to christen any of your six kids, or to be properly introduced to any of your six girlfriends. I felt hurt, Tom."

With his lawyer looking on in confusion, Tom twisted in his chair and entertained a flashback from his morning visit to his usual porn site.

Marl continued, "This time, Tom, you're looking at attempted robbery. Again . . ."

She shook her head and sighed, "Shit, Tom. If you had any

brains beyond the two feebles in your scrotum, you could copy-right that crime as your own. Think about it. You could conduct 3:00 A.M. infomercials and collect a monthly royalty check. But I digress . . ."

Tom's defense counsel sat up and cleared her throat to speak, only to be shushed by a wave of Marl's hand.

"Tom," she went on. "Most likely, on a good day, you'll be looking at three long in the Walpole State Penitentiary.

"You know Walpole, Tom. You spent six months there a couple of years ago. Nice place, isn't it? From what I hear, you were received like the belle at the debutant ball."

Tom stared at his lawyer while physically and mentally quivering.

Marl continued, "Tommy, don't look at her as your only possible savior in this small room. I can be an ally, too. I can be your friend."

She leaned forward and fixed her eyes on his. "May I be your friend, Tom?"

Marl could smell Tom's fear. She found the fumes nothing short of intoxicating.

Tom whispered sheepishly, "Y-Y-Yes. . . I th-think . . ."

"Excellent. I'll take that as your formal reply," said Marlene, as Tom's defense counsel just looked on, confused.

"See, Tom, my old friend," Marlene continued, "I heard that you actually volunteered some of your time to refereeing a few of the community basketball games. That was quite nice of you, Tom."

Tom just warily stared.

Marl recommenced, "Tom, of course we both know that any act of selfless kindness that you bestow upon this great city is done, of course, to serve your own self-interest and is, in fact, required of you by your probation officer.

"But so what? That's not against the rules. It's actually a smart move, Tom. Perhaps you're actually getting something through your thick, milk-chowder Irish skull. At any rate, I'm here to offer you a deal in consideration for your generous community service as well as one other small accommodation."

Tom's lawyer looked apprehensive, but she too was eager to hear Marlene's offer.

"So Tom," said Marlene, lightly tapping the table with her clasped hands. "I will formally drop all charges and cancel your one-way ticket to Walpole."

Tom remained motionless, apprehensive.

Marlene smiled. "Picture it, Tom. No 'Wal.' And more importantly, no 'Pole,' either"—she paused for dramatic effect before adding, "*if* you can do me a one little favor . . .

'off the grid,' so to speak."

At this point, one might expect Tom's attorney to slam her fist down and demand a meeting with the judge. This was not Wellesley, however. Not Marblehead. And not Lexington.

This was Boston. And the rules of the game were not only different, but downright contemptuous of how things worked in the civilized world. Boston not only invented its own unique system—it still enforced its values with an iron fist, and compassionate quarter was rarely shown.

"Tom," Marl continued. "There is this man. Actually he was a bit of a high school kissy/kissy friend, but that was a long time ago. Now, I'm afraid, he's a very bad man. Not bad to the extent that he should be sitting in our much-discussed Walpole prison, but a man who deserves to be taught an old-school Boston lesson nonetheless . . .

"Nothing crazy, Tom. You don't want to end up back here, and if you do I will deny everything while ensuring that you never make last call at Foley's ever again."

The hook was set. Tom was listening like he was hearing *Led Zeppelin Four* for the first time.

"Here's what I need you to do, Tom," Marlene went on. "Easy job. For you, it will come naturally. Like most people brushing their teeth. It'll be so normal that five minutes later you'll forget you even did it."

And with that bit of old-fashioned Beantown barter, John Tessio was to be greeted with a bad day just forty-eight hours later.

Tessio left his office at St. Eligius only to find that his Volvo sedan having had its tires slashed and its doors and hood thoroughly acquainted with quite a sharp key.

Stillness. Tessio was caught quite confused. As he ever so gently and slowly turned his head, out of deeply rooted instinct . . .

WHHAAPP!!!

In a moment of shock and disbelief, Tessio felt a fiercely directed club shatter his shoulder blade.

Only it was not an actual club. His twisted assailant had instead opted to use a miniature Red Sox souvenir bat, the kind of thing peddled to kids on Lansdowne Street.

Tessio fell to his knees in agony, shortly before said "child's toy" proceeded to slam into his other shoulder.

While John screamed and prayed to whatever deity he pretended to envision, his eyes were too flooded with tears to notice Tommy daftly deciding to take one more crack at the right shoulder, which shattered into fourteen pieces.

Fourteen? Now, that's a lot of pieces!

Tommy knew that he was getting carried away, and that perhaps the assistant district attorney would contend that his methodology was a bit extreme.

Meanwhile, John could not feel a thing in either arm. He was momentarily devoid of physical feeling or mental thought, for shock had moved in with a suitcase and planned on staying for a few weeks.

Tommy quickly turned away so that John would have no chance to see his face, and he proceeded to run through the parking garage and off into the night.

About ten minutes later, one of John's colleagues, in a state of complete disbelief, found him lying on the concrete floor, writhing and moaning in agony.

Within minutes, John was, well, back in the office—only this time it was in the ER, where he was tended to by a colleague whom John had only that very day shared the news of his upcoming layoff due to budget constraints.

Sometimes karma can arrive in the form of a dull needle.

You see, doctors can be the kindest of caregivers. However, you do not want them hanging over your body after a major injury if you have recently shown them the door to the unemployment line.

The doctor somehow forgot the correct dosage of painkiller as John clawed at the table with a raptorlike grip. To be sure, the doctor genuinely wondered about the crime that had produced this strange set of injuries. He wondered how long it would be before this poor bastard would be able to use his arms again. "Friggin' months," he quietly murmured to himself.

And back in Foley's pub, John's assailant, Tommy McInnen, also wondered at the strange set of attack instructions he had received from Marlene.

John Tessio was basically useless from his wrists to his shoulders. Unbeknownst to Tommy, Marl did not wish John Tessio dead or permanently maimed.

She just did not want him to be able to jerk off while convalescing . . .

Marlene at the Office of Shea & Rizzo

Marlene Dunn entered the office of S&R as briskly as if she were infiltrating Osama bin Laden's compound in Pakistan.

She approached the receptionist with the utmost swagger and said coldly, "Assistant District Attorney Marlene Dunn here to see Mr. Jester Chauncey. And no, I do not have an appointment."

The receptionist, quite taken aback and certainly not used to the authorities banging on the door, quickly picked up the phone. "Mr. Chauncey, there is an Assistant District Attorney Marlene Dunn here to see you."

Startled in his lair, Jester leaned back is his chair and breathed deeply. "Thank you. Please bring her in."

Moments later, Marl was greeted with a handshake that felt like a wounded haddock.

"Mr. Chauncey," she began curtly, without availing herself of the chair Jester was gesturing toward as he slumped back into his seat. "I've come here unofficially to extend the courtesy of informing you that the district attorney is investigating your firm with regard to BeamTech's trading practices. You must be aware of what I'm referring to, are you not?"

Jester shifted in his chair and glanced around at nothing in particular before answering, "Yes, and those trades are all clean. Counselor, you are barking up the wrong tree. We run a snow-white shop here. I would disagree that there exists any malfeasance."

Marlene retorted, "Well, it seems that you and your firm are wrapping silk sheets around a certain security and selling it to your clients as a gem, but from my office's perspective it has all the makings of a pump and dump.

"We will be in touch, Mr. Chauncey."

Chapter 16

Darby McBride

Darby was annoyed. It didn't take much to lift him to such an emotional state. Hot air traveled skyward.

Darb's thoughts swam back to a few days earlier, when he was not feeling himself (if there is such a state) and ended up going to see his doctor. Darby told her that his mental basement had been flooded out, and that he was still feeling depressed and listless.

Earlier in the year, his shrink had recommended that he start to dabble in some anti-depressant meds so that he might rejoin the euphoric fold.

Darby redarkened her doorway two months later angrily clutching an empty plastic Prozac bottle while screaming, "Fuckin' gained twenty pounds, packed with a limp dick to boot! The only crank with less fresh oil on it can be found under the hood of some rusted Pontiac in a Medford junkyard. This shit was supposed to make me *happy*, you head-shrinking twit!"

The doctor nodded with professional blankness.

Darb continued, "Those friggin' pills are supposed to part my clouds!? I'd rather be damned miserable, you sweaty thong!"

When the dust settled, the doctor went on the record to recommend sensitivity training, along with another scrip for twenty milligrams of "Fuck You."

Darby and Jus: Bal Harbour, Florida

Darb's mind returned to Earth just as Justin smashed his best Captain Quint impression.

"Y'all know me. You know what I do for a living . . ."

Darb was along for the Florida job as a consultant, and granted Jus the affirmation that he was strong in character.

Jus had to be careful. He needed to get very close to this target. He regretted having to "remove" said target on his family vacation, but duty called and Jus loved playing around with his fake accents, trying to bring them to perfection.

This particular target was an Orthodox Jew, which was indeed a new one for Jus (though he did certainly believe in celebrating diversity—Jus was an equal-opportunity offender, to be sure).

Jus's bet was that this guy was genuine. A true believer in his faith, someone who held tradition sacred. Jus did buy that. From that moment on, for his own purposes Jus would refer to the Orthodox merely as "Target."

Target's father had built from the first brick an amazing shipping network that ran from New York City to Tel Aviv, with a very lucrative port of call in London. It was all legitimate, and Target's father was a good man. Some of his peers referred to him as a veritable *tzadik*.

Yet Target, the son, was spoiled rotten, and his arrogance unfortunately led him to stretch the organization's practices beyond the boundaries of acceptable international trade policy.

No, not drugs. That was a dirty business and beneath the likes of Target. Instead, Target unabashedly ran guns—Old Russian hardware that proved quite popular on the black market. That particular world of trade jolted him like a syringe of cooked brown laced with Cialis.

He needed no hole in the sheet to send him to the ecstasy . . .

So Target formed a relationship with a few "untouchables" known to the underworld as the IRA. Their product came from some Central American jungle.

The weapons were stowed in weather-beaten crates that were transported on Target's boats, which conveniently made an unscheduled "repair anchorage" off the coast of the Emerald Isle for twelve hours or so.

While the rest of the zombie tourists were touring the Ring of Kerry and waiting in line to kiss the Blarney Stone (which is said to be pissed on by local teenagers after closing time), Target and his band of coat-holders were busy unloading automatic weapons and ammunition onto some of the local fishing vessels.

Target was proud of himself. Although he certainly did reap a significant profit from his enterprise, he also made generous donations to help fund Israeli covert operations. Over time, Target's ego mushroomed like the Jornada del Muerto desert on July 16, 1945. You see, Target failed to notice any curious irony to the whole operation.

You can put a nice Christmas sweater on a mangy pit bull, but it's still a cur.

All was moving along smoothly for quite some time, until certain "interested parties" in Boston were beginning to see an erosion of their market share in the IRA weapons trade, and rumors were spreading about an "outsider" to the business moving in under the guise of his hard-working father's honest and successful enterprise.

That was when Darby McBride's cell phone awoke. Darb noticed the number and suddenly the light on the phone shone as brightly as an old-school blast of fireworks over the moonlit Charles River on the Fourth of July.

Darby was given a description of the situation and immediately knew just the candidate for the assignment. Justin McGee would fit right in with the cocktail-hour crowd at an Oscar de la Renta opening at the Bal Harbour Shops, yet he could quickly mutate into various characters who might be easy enough for witnesses to remember, but certainly difficult for them ever to see Jus in such a role again.

And certainly not in a police line-up . . .

As soon as Darby had the details from his client he immediately dialed Jus, who listened intently, especially to the part about the payout if the job was successful.

In fact, Jus listened so intently that, when something caused him to stir a bit, he noticed with a quick little giggle that there was saliva dripping into the guts of his phone, threatening to short the circuits.

Darby

Prior to heading to Florida for reconnaissance with Jus, Darby found himself in a self-induced mental and emotional state as thick as a New England fog bank.

He felt like the proverbial hamster on a wheel that has been desperately striving to catch up with a piece of cheese for the better part of sixty-five years.

The upcoming trip to Florida was a bit jarring. He knew that it was a great opportunity, but he realized that these jobs for "veterans" of the business in Boston were indeed drying up. By Darb's estimation, the Hub would resemble Death Valley in five years, opportunity-wise.

A little reluctantly, he decided to consult Mahoney—an old friend and semi-mentor from whom he had learned, via direct observation and general osmosis, so much about "the life" when he was a kid. At age seventy-five, Mahoney had ten years on Darby and had lived a hard life, and thus was well into his retirement—if there exists such a status in that particular industry.

Darb pulled into the parking lot of Pine Hills Assisted Living Center, and found that there were plenty of spaces available right near the main entrance. Apparently, the residents of said institution did not receive all that many regular visitors.

He walked in and greeted the well-dressed, smiling Latina hostess/ receptionist and was directed to Mahoney's room.

As Darb slowly entered the room—you never startled Mahoney, not even during a so-called dormant retirement—he peered inside and saw the aging gangster calmly staring at what looked like a crossword puzzle book while holding a silver Cross pen. Years of a self-inflicted, punishing lifestyle had made him look at least ten years older than he really was.

Mahoney immediately looked up, and with a crooked smile he said, "Darby McBride. Sonofabitch. . . It's been quite a while. You must be in trouble, and no, I can't float you a loan. This damn place is robbing me blind of both soul and wallet."

Darb responded, "No, Mahoney. I just stopped by to say hello. Ya know, see how you're doing and all of that happy horseshit."

"Bullshit, Darb. You're in some kind of jam. You're not the kind of selfish bastard to make a social call to an aging bigger selfish bastard. What's the rumpus?"

"Well, Mahoney . . . I gotta make a trip to South Florida with a *protégé* of mine in order to set up a job. Sort of a . . . terminal job. Anyway, it just got me thinking . . . well, more like lamenting. What the hell has happened to our world? Our contacts. Our code. Our boys. Our way of 'doing things and getting things done'? I find that I now have to travel three hours by plane in order to find any decent work. How can an honest player make a dishonest living anymore? What's the world coming to?"

Mahoney shook his head sadly.

"Your generation had it all figured out," Darby continued. "You kept it in the neighborhood, and either kicked or kissed ass when particular situations presented themselves. There was order. There was a hierarchy, and every swinging dick knew where he stood and where his place was in the pecking order. And if some wise-ass bastard got out of line, he was taken behind the shed, and 95 percent of the time it was well-deserved and expected by his peers."

Mahoney barely nodded.

"There's none of that anymore," Darby went on. "It's the Wild West, and the damn Injuns are running the prairie."

Mahoney leaned back in his chair and adjusted the blanket around the dry, papery skin of his frail legs. "Darb," he said with a tired, raspy voice. "The life we chose was a unique one. One that provided us with an exciting and lucrative living. However, nobody ever guaranteed that it was permanent. Things change. Conditions evolve, and eventually you find that the way that we did things most likely belongs in a museum exhibit or a Ken Burns documentary."

He paused for effect, and then continued, "We had a great run, Darb. Guys made a lot of money, banged a lot of broads, and life was good. Cops left us alone—shit, they became partners."

Darby nodded, chuckling.

"But the world evolves, Darb," Mahoney went on. "Look at me—I lived hard and I get it—I'm resigned to the fact that and the world is going to swallow me soon."

For a few moments, the only sounds were Mahoney's coarse, irregular breathing and the murmur of the televisions in nearby rooms.

Mahoney gestured at Darby with a bony finger. "You're hanging on to a past life and a culture that no longer exists. In some ways I admire you for keeping the torch lit, but at the same time I pity you for being so naive."

Darby stood stock-still, saying nothing. What could he say?

Mahoney gazed blankly out the window for a moment, then back at his old associate. "Darb, our friends are all defunct—they're either in prison or 'feeding the tree.' If you still want to brandish the sword, then all I can suggest is that you give it hell and go down swinging."

Mahoney paused, then fumbled with the straw protruding from a plastic cup of water. After taking a pull, he carefully set the cup back down and, without looking up at Darby, he said, "This lamenting of yours is doing you no good, my friend, nor is it doing your predecessors any favors or giving them proper respect in any way. Just follow your gut and savor each breath on the road like it will be your last—'cause someday it will be. Someday sooner than you think."

At that point, an Italian would have kissed Mahoney's hand. The Irish, however, did not embrace such flitty customs.

Instead, Darb bowed slightly and quietly wished Mahoney the best of health.

As he walked out of the room, Darb considered that, while the older man may be slowly losing the body that he had put through so much, the mind that he had worked even harder was still purring like a vintage candy-apple-red Corvette.

Chapter 17

Jus

Jus never forgot a lover.

He craved the touch. The connection, the soft, hair-dryer breathing.

He was perpetually at war with himself, and so the desire for wonton connection and the desire for companionship would escort one another to the dance in his head.

Sometimes Jus would find himself daydreaming about an old roommate. Actually, he wasn't sure if it was a dream, and in adulthood he chocked it up to doubling down on his Ativan scrip.

Pills were a game. Smash one set with a rubber hammer and two more would arrive in his palm.

Even from an early age, Jus had always had very vocal internal roommates. It was strange for a child who was so self-absorbed—how could he share the microphone with blurry visions born of his own advanced imagination?

He would often ponder this and his mind would immediately go squirrel.

One of these damn internal roommates used to color all day. Color and color and color—crayons, water color paints, and a Skittles bag of magic-marker colors. While he found relaxation in all of the colors, for some innate reason red always gripped him with the most intensity. That crayon would quickly wear out, which Jus interpreted as illustrating the fleeting nature of the world around him. Sometimes in a dream, a crayon in a nondescript color would melt into a brilliant red then slowly mix with a subtle brown that invariably brought on that smell of copper.

Jus could have made a fortune as a Crayola consultant once they went to scented crayons . . .

He dreamed of floating shells. A day on the beach with the beautiful children that he would never have. The shells would begin to sink, even though Jus would dive into the water to prevent that inevitable occurrence.

Yet for Jus, the shells always sank eventually.

No, he wasn't Holden Caulfield. He just dreamed of the children who never would look into his eyes, and whose delusional thoughts and memories would leave him staring at vapor trails that were meant to be burning skid marks etched on stubborn gray pavement.

For Jus spent so much time dealing in death and strategizing over the ways of wealth that he rarely pulled over into a mental rest area and contemplated what he was really lacking.

He had a life that some would certainly covet—indeed, they would jump on it like a fumble on the one-yard line. But Jus's inner state, once bright with rainbow tones, was now bleaching out and morphing into a limp and pallid gray. He missed the Sunday-morning cuddle, and reaching over the sheets to find a casual conversation that would set the tone for the day ahead. He missed putting on the news while gently and yet firmly holding the one he loved. Connection would be established and soft love-making would ensue.

Dreams . . .

For Jus, they were the most perverse and painful type of lies.

Jus and Meyer: Before the Florida Job

Meyer knew exactly where Jus snagged his lunch every day—a small deli off of Broad Street in the Financial District where he would always get fresh soup and a salad. Jus always ate well, and it certainly worked for luring beautiful lassies back to his condo for pleasant afternoons.

Jus's only vices were the occasional Kit Kat and Ketel One apple martini.

As Meyer rolled in he openly cursed—on purpose, within ear shot of the owner—that the damned doorway was "too fuckin' narrow for a poor crippled eggplant."

The joint had been there so long that it had a grandfathered-in exemption from the recently enacted disability laws.

Meyer moved a chair aside and wheeled himself up to the table. The old friends exchanged salutations, nothing too dramatic. Meyer knew when Jus's wheels were turning, and he knew exactly what that meant.

"Hey, Jus," quipped Meyer. "When are you going to settle down with a nice girl? You know—kids, barbecues, soccer tryouts . . . the whole dream . . ."

Jus couldn't help but render a half-smile / half-frown, and answered, "I don't know, old friend—I sincerely doubt that it's in the cards. Guys like me don't stand over a grill or stir potato salad. And my version of playing cornhole is rather different than that of your average suburban window-dressing family . . ."

Meyer nodded, chuckling.

"Yeah," Jus went on, "I guess that you and me both are gonna ski the singles chairlift lines at our respective mountains until they have to drag us down the hill in a sled."

Meyer changed the air. "Jus. I know how you get when you are considering a new 'assignment.' What do you have to do? Too risky? Your head seems very heavy on this one."

Jus leaned back with a deep sigh. "The risks are always there," he said. "It's just that I'm not getting any younger, and I want to make sure that I don't overstay my welcome in an industry that constantly spawns younger, more eager, more fucked-up lunatics"

While Jus, at the ripe old age of thirty-eight, wasn't exactly long in the tooth, Meyer knew exactly what he meant. An assassin had about the same useful lifespan as an NFL quarterback.

"Hey, Jus—most of the guys entering the 'industry' are cowboys supporting a coke habit. How many of them possess even a feeble iota of a brain? How many of them can hide behind a successful law practice? They hang out in bars all day getting drunk and subsequently they shoot their mouths off. Why do you think your services are in such high demand?"

Jus said nothing.

Meyer continued, "Perhaps it's time to consider taking on a partner? You know—someone to maybe provide some ground recon while you're setting things up?"

Jus bobbed his head noncommittally and said, "I dunno, man— that could make some sense, but I don't want to split the money . . . and moreover I don't trust anyone."

Meyer leaned forward. "Do you trust me, Jus?"

Jus responded with a skeptical look. "Wait a minute," he said. "What do you think you would do? Provide recon within a hundred feet of the hit, and then strap a rocket to the back of your wheelchair and blast away at light speed to escape the target's bodyguard's sawed-off?" He shook his head. "C'mon, man—you're going soft! Stick to marathons and conquering the chin-up bar in the weight room, and Route One strippers . . ."

It was true. From the waist up, Meyer was, pound for pound, just about the strongest man Jus had ever met. And this was no gift from Mother Nature. It came from grueling work, and a mental fortitude that left anyone who knew him feeling like a sloth.

"Jus," said Meyer in a low, direct voice. "Who's going to take a potshot at a poor, homeless darkie in a wheelchair who just so happens to be in the neighborhood collecting cans when suddenly a hit goes down?"

He paused, seeing that the wheels were turning in Justin's head.

"Nobody will be the wiser," Meyer went on. "It's a perfect plan. I can pretend to be crazy, which won't be much of a stretch. I can talk to myself, but in reality I'm keeping you informed of the target's movements via a small two-way radio. We can develop an easy code—we won't need many words. I'll carry a small semi-automatic, for which I am licensed thanks to my military service, just in case shit goes hurricane . . ."

Jus still could not believe this proposition. And yet, as usual, Meyer was providing sage counsel and innovative ideas that might not be so outlandish after all.

But Jus was still skeptical. "How about money, Meyer?" he asked. "I'm sure that you don't want to risk your life for gratis, nor should you. At the same time, the work is getting more and more dangerous, and I do like my payday."

Meyer replied, "Actually, I'm not doing it for the money. Jus, I need a little action in my life! Shit—a few years ago I was carrying an M16 and fighting dirtbag terrorists who threatened our country, and I was damn proud of it."

Meyer could see that he was making his point. He went on, "The way I look at it, I'm helping you take out scumbags of a different profile. I would suggest that if I'm no help to the hit, and that you did it completely on your own, I wouldn't want any excessive compensation. I would only request a mere 5 percent for incidental expenses incurred during setting up the project."

Justin's face betrayed neither agreement nor disagreement, so Meyer continued to press his case. "However," he said, "if I can provide intel to save your ass and make a job a success, I would consider 25 percent to be a fair cut. And quite generous on my end, if I may dare say. I would trust you to be the judge as to the value of my services."

After a long pause, Jus replied, "How are you going to convince them that you are some lowly street cripple?"

Meyer had an easy answer. "Remember all of those nonsense drama classes and theater groups that I participated in when we were in school? Anything to be around a lot of broads and not go to a real class. Well, the only role they'll offer me going forward is fuckin' Tiny Tim, so maybe I can dust off my acting skills and find that zone again."

Meyer saw a faint smile come to Jus's face, so he continued, "Shit, man, we could be a hell of a tag team, you know, like wrestlers, like

Tony Garea and Rick Martel. It could be better than you having friggin' Johnny Martorano in your corner . . ."

Jus wasn't quite convinced of that, but at the same time he was intrigued, for it would take Martorano about three seconds to be "made" by the underworld ilk, while Meyer could certainly maintain a much lower profile.

Still, Jus was in no hurry to put his best friend in such danger. Meyer's approach did have its merits, true, but his proposal had to be weighed slowly and methodically, which is the sentiment that he relayed to Meyer.

Jus wasn't ruling it out, for it could be a more efficient and effective way to execute a job—with *execute* being the operative word.

Jus was quiet for a long time, and Meyer knew not to say another word.

Suddenly Jus said, "Hey, Meyer. I was talking to Darby and he has a client who is starting to dabble in all of this kinky underground porn-movie shit. Fancies himself a modern-day Russ Meyer–type of director."

Jus arched his eyebrows, and they both laughed.

"Anyway," he went on, "his new skin flick is what he claims will be a high-quality, all-blaxploition piece, with a few white college chicks thrown in to keep the downloads moving. He's calling it *Urban Sprawl*. . . And most importantly, he needs a handsome, athletic stud to assume the starring role. Why not run with something like that?"

Meyer responded with a polite "Go F yourself."

Jus loved Meyer like a brother, and he knew how to push his buttons in order to get an entertaining rise out of the very disciplined former military man. It was true that, although Meyer was uniquely successful as a soldier and athlete, he sometimes struggled with his career and other facets of his life that threatened his keen sense of self-confidence and swagger. While his best friends enjoyed their self-indulgent lives and careers, he found himself faced with an incredibly difficult task of gradual re-entry into the contemporary workplace. Even though Meyer was most comfortable in any environment where orders were clearly given and followed without question or discussion, nevertheless he bitterly resented having to take orders from some bloated, fat-cat, middle-management type.

At one point he was desperately looking for any job that came with decent health insurance. Of course, as a disabled veteran, Meyer was eligible for VA benefits, but what the public didn't realize was that government-provided health care was not exactly on par with the Cadillac Blue Cross plans of the 1990s.

Meyer was offered and subsequently accepted a position with a politically active tax advocacy group known as PAKRA, which proudly stood for "People for A Kinder Reach-Around."

They were a typical clandestine liberal think-tank that posed as fighting for the cause of the taxpaying voters, but in the end PAKRA really just wanted to convince the hard-working citizens of Massachusetts that paying taxes is a small price to pay for the privilege of living in this great nation, and that their organization would look out for their best interests.

Meyer would often bitterly tell the story of how he realized that the job offer was obviously based on his "condition" and not his skills. PAKRA had just celebrated a victory; they had successfully lobbied the Massachusetts state legislature to pass a bill calling for state funding of a study to consider the pros and cons of developing a scientific process for sex changes in cats. It seems that cats were becoming confused as to their gender identity, and PAKRA wanted to be on the front lines of this pressing issue that was perceived by them to be at the forefront of the concerns of the average working-class voter.

At any rate, some members of the media requested a site visit to PAKRA's headquarters in Newton, and of course they wanted a Q&A, complete with a group photo-op.

The program's director, who called himself Tink, had hand-picked the all-stars within his group to serve as the illustrative photographic representation of his team's efforts. Meyer was included, even though he had joined the crew well after PAKRA's efforts to sway the local reps on the cat issue. Not to mention the fact that Meyer thought that the piece of legislation in question was the equivalent of a circus playbill.

It did not take long for Meyer to realize that his inclusion in the photo shoot was solely for PAKRA to be able to tout that the organization employed and sought the advice and involvement of an Iraq War veteran who was permanently wounded, and who also happened to be black. To Tink, that was the equivalent to a trifecta at Suffolk Downs—kind of like finding the fake tattoo kit at the bottom of the Cracker Jack box.

Unfortunately for Tink, Meyer did not take this well. As soon as the press people had packed up and gone, Meyer wheeled himself right up to the director's desk after firmly shutting the office door, and he confronted Tink about making him a star in this media piece. Tink, in his never-ending state of integrity and bravado, denied any such ill intention.

The snow globe that had long graced Tink's desk (it was a gift from his niece who was currently in the Philippines teaching haiku to an indigenous tribe that had embraced Islamic terrorism and needed to be "understood") caught the director's nose at its longest point. Meyer still had quite a fast ball.

This immediately caused a chain reaction—a crunch of cartilage, a schoolgirl squeal, and a red stream down Tink's paisley bow tie.

Meyer quietly placed the now-blood-stained ornament back onto Tink's desk, and quietly wheeled himself out of the room after calmly and politely tendering his resignation. Meyer felt no fear of retribution of arrest due to his exploits, for who's gonna hear a case where a trust-fund suburban soft-skin presses charges against a minority wounded war vet?

For once, Meyer embraced political correctness, and he quietly belly-laughed at the spark of enlightenment . . .

Meyer noticed that Justin had barely touched his soup. *Maybe*, he thought to himself, that *starring role in* Urban Sprawl *didn't seem so bad after all.*

Meanwhile, Jus was thinking that Meyer had better be a friggin' Pacino of an actor, or he would never enjoy another track workout after the first hit attempt.

Jus had an idea . . .

Jus and Darby: On the Set of *Urban Sprawl*

The seventies funk music cranking in the background was pure aural sandpaper to Darby McBride. As he gazed around, he felt like he was living a dream where he was dropped from a helicopter onto the set of *Good Times*, yet he had to keep reminding himself that he was indeed "working" and representing a client.

This particular scene evoked both a chuckle and an eye-roll from ol' Darb. The backdrop was a boxing ring in a large auditorium. In one corner of the ring were two extremely hot college girls, one black and one white, who were wearing boxing gloves. Just boxing gloves.

Suddenly, the director called for action and the fans—about a dozen college kids who had been fiddling with their cell phones—went wild. A loudspeaker began to blare out a rockin' tune called "Mike Spinks!" played to the tune of "Love Stinks," the old J. Giles Band song. Entering the other side of the ring was a male actor who bore the uncanny resemblance to Smokin' Joe Frazier at the prime of his career.

Meanwhile, Darb just shook his head as Jus came through the studio door.

Darby was always ice.

Without really looking at his younger *protégé*, he said, "You ready for this one, Jus?"

Jus returned with "Yeah, this should be a layup. The Ocean View Hotel in Bal Harbour is thin and tall. The top floor provides a good panoramic vantage point overlooking the pool and beach area."

Darby nodded impassively.

Jus continued, "I'll make the stab and be down the stairs and into the car before anyone realizes that it wasn't a sudden heart attack . . ."

Jus planned on using very small-caliber bullets, which would not produce much blood. Some hits were purposely set up for dramatic effect. This was not one of them, for Target's family was expected to be present.

"I'll drive up to Atlanta over the next several hours," Jus went on, "and get lost in that clusterfuck of an airport. Should be back in Boston not too long thereafter if all goes smooth."

Damn, this job is getting old, Jus thought to himself.

As if reading his mind, Darby quipped, "Hey, Jus—think of it as just another day at the office."

Jus took great pride in his professionalism, in seeing to it that his trade was always properly plied. His greatest fear was that he might actually take on an assignment and enjoy it. He never killed for sport or vengeance, for those were the actions of the animals and the unenlightened.

Such people did not hold prestigious jobs, or bed insatiable women. They were just soulless killers, and Jus would not be lumped into that pile of unintelligent vermin.

Well.

Maybe just once.

Youth is a once-in-a-lifetime asset, but it can be squandered and rendered dangerous when it takes the dance floor to request that the band play a song of retribution.

Darby pulled out another toothpick and said, "Hey—when you get home, as a bonus I might have a little tip for you regarding a little piece of light work in Gloucester . . ."

Flash Back Fifteen Years: Jamaica

Jus was a younger man at the time. He always dreamed of a Spring Break trip with his college cronies. Perhaps he had seen too many National Lampoon movies.

Jus's group took a cheap flight south in the late-hour darkness.

Upon landing in Montego Bay, Jus realized that it was one o'clock in the morning. All were exhausted, yet still reeling from adrenaline and mile-high drinking.

Their "chariot" to the hotel picked them up and proceeded toward
their destination in Negril. Several in Jus's party were slowly beginning
to nod off, when all of a sudden there was a screeching of brakes and
the scratch of tires on gravel.

They found themselves at the Jamaican version of a "rest area" at
2:00 A.M.

What had been, a moment before, just the barren crust of a building
on the side of the road suddenly blazed with light, music, and laughter.
Jus needed this. He needed to escape from the fear of his upcoming
graduation, the fear of growing up, the fear of succeeding (whatever
that might mean), and the fear that he would have to make some feeble
attempt at self-actualization.

But at the moment, what Jus really needed was a little extra money.

As is customary at a Jamaican roadside stop-off in the middle of the
night, the market was alive with vendors representing the diversity of
the Jamaican tourist economy.

A line around one hut was for the Rasta selling kind bud (*How
original*, thought Jus—*at least there's nothing stereotypical here in this
country*). Another vendor, whose presence was by far the most popular
with the group, was willing to share Red Stripe beer at half-price.

But there was another alleyway that led to two Rastas who were
looking for American gold.

Any American gold.

Commodity speculators, thought Jus at even such a young age.

With a stinging reek of pot smoke and sweat invading his nostrils,
Jus walked up and presented a gold chain that was given to him by
the most attractive, siren-like woman in his life, who had broken his
heart a few months earlier.

He hated to part with it, but she had decided to part with him
and toss Jus into the outgoing tide, so he figured he would engage in
good ol'-fashioned capitalism in the middle of the night on the road
to Negril.

The Rasta spoke: "Eees this real, mon?"

Great, thought Jus. *A Caribbean commodity broker . . .*

"Geeeve you fitty bocks, mon . . ."

"Sh-sh-sure . . . ," Jus responded.

"Eef this not reeel, mon, I know where you stay. Me cousin drive the bus, mon. . . He know where you stay."

Jus saw where this was going. *Yeah, yeah. Microeconomics . . .*

He suddenly felt the handgun against his temple as his partner in barter reminded him that this piece of jewelry had better be real.

Jus did not take well to any such physical threat, notwithstanding the fact that he really had no idea if the damn necklace would immediately turn lime-green once immersed in the salty Caribbean.

The only problem was that Jus was not wired like the usual college snot-nose.

Jus took his fifty bucks for the gold. *That's a solid day's drinking money*, he thought, *and might even cover a feeble meal.*

Jus headed back to the bus as the rest of the tourists continued to barter.

No, this was not the friggin' 1970s *Love Boat* stop at Puerto Vallarta . . .

Jus approached the bus driver as the last vapor trails emitted from his nose. "Hey," he said, "I just did some business with your cousin and he said that there are more deals to be had. Well, funny thing. If you are looking for gold, I have a group of friends who are flying in on a charter and would love to lose some weight in exchange for some scratch."

This was *the* most innocent, pathetic transaction that the bus driver had ever heard of, but he was stoned to the gills and wanted to respond to the prospect of some easy American gold to be resold at a profit—and better yet, the prospect of access to the tourist resorts and pools.

"Okay, mon," he said. "What time would you like me to be there? My name is Terio. My name is Terio The Driver."

"Hello Terio The Driver," responded Jus. "Your cousin got a little fresh with me over there. Who runs this operation? Did you just happen to bring us here by accident?"

To which Terio had to emit a soft chuckle. "No, mon. This whole place is my operation. If me cousin got a little rough with you, it 'cause that's just his nature and how he was born and raised. He doesn't have the brain capacity required to split open a coconut with the sharpest machete on the island. No, mon, but he is quite versed in the ways of violence and getting things done, all while watching you rich, white American boys frightened when a real Jamaican man make you quiver in your fancy shoes. And I also must admit that he maintains quite a track record for causing many an American drunken white wise-ass a lot of physical pain. You are lucky that you don't have a black eye, broken arm or worse."

Jus knew that the guy who five minutes earlier had put the hand-gun to his temple was bad news, and who knows how many tourists he had robbed, cheated, beaten, or worse. Terio's cousin was not an asset to this planet.

Jus rubbed his chin. "Mr. Terio, sir, you see if I bring you lots of American gold for you to purchase at a discounted rate, I would also like to wet my beak for putting the deal together. Not huge money, but might we be able to make this work for, say, 20 percent of the total value of the transactions for my white ass?"

Terio laughed. "He with the white ass never gets 20 percent in Jamaica—ya sniffin' glue, mon . . ."

Jus responded, "Okay. Ten to me. After all, I'm in your backyard, and I intend to show the proper respect that is deserved. That's the least that I can do."

Terio The Driver nodded. "See you, then," he said. "But my cousin go by himself, mon. I need not be there for such a light assignment, mon."

"That would be great," said a plotting Justin. "Just send your cousin alone. We can do business and hopefully be friends."

And with that, the two exchanged the traditional Jamaican fist tap. A sign of respect . . .

The two arranged a time and place for Jus and Terio's cousin to consummate their transaction.

Unbeknownst to Terio, he had just sealed his cousin's fate. The fact that the next time Jus came face to face with the Rasta who had threatened his life would be a very bad day for said Jamaican cousin, and Jus simply needed to figure out how to bring the deed to fruition.

Jus did not respond well to threats . . .

Present Day: Bal Harbour, Florida

Jus slowly mounted the Old World hardwood stairs of the stately Ocean View Hotel. The joint had a storied history, boasted a guest list that, over the years, included sultans, heads of state, captains of industry, and some of the most elite politicians and power brokers the country had ever seen.

Before seeking out the highest ground, Jus felt that a glass of wine might calm his nerves, which perhaps would be an asset to all involved. After all, it was in everyone's best interest that Jus maintain his record of total accuracy.

Jus was a bit scared, as he knew he should be.

He walked into the bar and engaged the usual type. "Just wondering if I may have a Pinot Grigio, please?"

Some guys would feel quite insecure about ordering a white wine if they were alone in a bar full of strangers, but Jus had stopped trying to prove anything a lifetime ago.

A waiter asked Jus to move to the deck because there was some kind of marital event underway, and he was not invited to participate. The man made it quite explicitly clear that Jus was a second-class citizen who was not invited to this particular ball.

Big mistake—Jus did not appreciate being relegated to said deck. But lucky for the waiter, the assassin was already quite preoccupied that particular afternoon. The stress was falling over him like New Year's Eve confetti.

The waters in his head began rising . . .

He was quickly thrust into assassin mode.

He walked methodically and deliberately. The closer that he got to the roof, the more his animal instinct took over and his adrenaline surged.

Yet this was his calling. This was his born-to vocation. He passed a beautiful young mom with a darling daughter who was afraid of elevators. As was Jus . . .

Upon reaching the roof, he took a moment to gaze upon the azure of the gentle Atlantic Ocean. It was a soft day with very little wind. Jus was as transfixed by the beauty of the scene as he had been by that sparkling diamond of a woman in the hallway, and with a smirk he had to admit to himself that there was nothing like an intensely pretty woman to render a man aimless.

But back to business.

He lay down his duffle bag and began to assemble the tool of his trade.

For a passing moment, he "almost" felt an iota of remorse. But that passed quickly as he spotted Target down below, sticking his feet in the pool.

Jus quietly placed the rifle on the rough-edged white concrete of the parapet wall that encircled the roof. His finger gently caressed the trigger. If only he felt this passion and connection toward other components of his life.

He slowly and methodically peered into the high-powered scope and watched as Target scolded his *shiksa* wife.

The first shot rendered no noise. The first shot was always the quietest. And as always, it produced just a confused look on the recipient, who immediately assumed he'd been stung by a wasp.

The second shot removed sections of the unsuspecting head, and the subsequent explosive noise only magnified the most primal of human recognitions.

Jamaica: 2001

As Rasta pulled into the abandoned motel's parking lot at around 3:00 A.M., Jus lay quietly waiting behind a gently swaying colony of palm trees.

Rasta slowly got out of his car and slowly peered around the vast, deserted, unlit emptiness.

Jus could see that Rasta was somewhat confused, as he was expecting a group of drunken, over-partied college kids eager to barter away their valuables in order to be able to score another elbow of some fine Jamaican weed.

Rasta wore a loose-fitting distressed paisley button-down shirt, which draped around his near-emaciated figure. The only contour of his body was the thick bulge of the 9-millimeter tucked into his belt, overtly displayed as a reminder that he was actually not "alone."

Jus did not want to startle Rasta but to surprise him gently, while simultaneously keeping him at ease.

"Hey mon," Jus whispered loudly.

Rasta turned and for a brief instant lightly tapped his finger on his weapon, as if by instinct.

"Mon . . . I see you again, but I no see your friends. . . Where eeze the gold?" (He pronounced it "gode," of course.)

"Sorry, my friend," Jus replied. "I hope that this wasn't a wasted trip for you. My friends spent too much time pulling tube in the sun today, and they're all passed out. So it's just me, but I do have a really nice bracelet that you may be interested in. I'm firm on my price of one hundred J."

Rasta chuckled. "One hondred J. . . Bettah be a nice piece, mon."

As the two approached each other, Jus gingerly made certain that the buck knife he had purchased the day before at the open market was still snugged in the back of the waist of his shorts.

This was going to be dicey, and it had to be executed extremely quickly and with furious abandon. Still, there was a part of Jus that inherently knew that although he was treading in Rasta's jungle, Jus was really the predator this evening.

The two exchanged fist taps. "Respect," each said simultaneously.

With that, Jus held out the gold bracelet (also purchased at the open market for five bucks—it was clearly made of tin). Jus already had the trinket in his hand, for he did not want to put Rasta on edge by having to reach into his pocket.

"Lemme see, mon." With that, Rasta reached out and took the

bracelet from Jus and held it up to the moonlight so as to judge the piece's integrity.

The lack of illumination worked in Jus's favor, for upon a proper inspection, anyone could have seen clearly that this jewelry might have rolled out of a fifty-cent gumball machine.

As Rasta viewed the pseudo bling, a profound serenity came over Jus. Nearly anyone's blood would surge and their heart would race at this moment, but Jus only felt a strange sense of calmness. Peace . . .

As his heart rate strangely slowed to a meditative calm, and as Rasta stared upward at the moonlight to better see the faux bracelet, Jus in a split second freed the buck knife from the confines of his waistband and in one swift, arcing movement diced it across Rasta's abdomen, eviscerating him. Rasta's draping shirt, which only a few seconds before had been devoid of any true color, was immediately painted a deep crimson.

Strangely, there were no shrieks of horror. No yelling or cursing. Actually, there was no sound at all to stir the sea of birds nestled in the trees around them. All that was present was a confused look of disbelief on Rasta's face.

Before Rasta fell to the ground, Jus relieved him of his pistol, held it to Rasta's head, and calmly squeezed the trigger. Immediately all of the hopes, dreams, swagger, and mojo swam away from Rasta's abandoned barge of a soul.

Jus stared. He then emitted a slight chuckle at the vision of one particular Easter during his childhood. He always found it amazing how the mind could so quickly play back a two-hour reel of film in a nanosecond.

The catalyst for the flashback was the uncanny resemblance of what remained of Rasta's head to the inside of a Cadbury Cream Egg . . .

But Jus knew that time was short. He dragged Rasta's rag-doll body into the scrub weeds and did his best to conceal this unique adventure.

He knew that the Jamaican authorities were unlikely to initiate a nationwide search for Rasta's killer, for the tourism trade was the lifeblood of this tumultuous country, and news of any kind of violence coming out of Jamaica would mean grumbling travel agents and barren stools at the swim-up bars.

No, tracking down the killer of one dead local thug was not worth the prospect of dollar-throwing tourists avoiding this particular rock and instead opting for tacky Cancun or insipid Nassau. The Jamaican government would just as soon keep those plump American asses in the seats of Air Jamaica's jet planes, thank you.

Nevertheless, Jus also knew that the smart thing to do was to not take any chances and to get off of this particular rock immediately—this spring break getaway was over. There was no going back to his Red Stripe buddies, no going back to the reggae beach concerts, and no going back to flirting with the ebony gems pouring the rum punch at the beach bars.

Next stop was the airport in Montego Bay, where he could catch the first flight out to anywhere stateside.

Such was Jus's truth at this particular moment in time. There was no going back. . . In any way.

Chapter 18

Present Day: Jus's Daydream of Seeing Marlene

Justin felt embarrassingly like a stalker, even though he had long ago mastered a professional assassin's skills at moving around unnoticed.

He always entered a room as if walking onto the set of *Terminator 2*. Without exception, he would immediately scan the room first from left to right, as if reading a printed text, and then again in the opposite direction.

While some may view it as a trait of a skillful hunter, to Jus it was more of a curse that needed to be both explored and expunged.

To him it was maddening. All he wanted to do was to order a damn sandwich!

As Jus walked through the popular lunch spot with a Cobain look of "Here I am now, entertain me . . . ," his usual room-scanning suddenly flooded brain tubes one and two.

His dirty, three-day old contact lenses revealed a stunning vision. Graceful. Slow-moving. Dress flowing with every swaying motion to port or starboard.

Suddenly the woman wearing the dress yelled, "Gimme an Italian with no hots!"

From behind the counter came the habitual bellowed response: "All Italians have hots, Honey!"—which of course was greeted with roars of laughter from the other workers.

To Jus, this appeared to be just the usual banter between said customer and the jovial guy slicing tomatoes. Jus took it all in and then brazenly approached the strikingly attractive woman, and—as only Jus could be so arrogant—said, "Between the Ann Taylor gear and the berating of the staff, I have you pegged as a ruthless prosecutor . . ."

The woman calmly replied, "Who is asking, and why the fuck should I feel any need to respond?"

"No response needed, m'dear, and your hostile reaction is quite unnecessary. It was more that I was drawn to how you ordered that sandwich, as if you were crushing a hostile witness."

For one—*one*—brief moment, Marlene Dunn felt vulnerable for the first time in her life. For Marlene, exposure was tantamount to weakness.

Justin instinctively sensed that passing flash of weakness. For him, this vulnerability was an invitation to explore the most intoxicatingly beautiful woman he had ever seen. And he certainly had seen plenty . . .

To Jus, a beautiful woman's anger was the ultimate turn-on.

And Marlene was pissed. Just profoundly pissed.

Marlene used to get exactly this pissed at her slob brothers.

No, not the usual slovenliness to be expected from a houseful of lower-middle-class Boston Irish boys.

Yes, of course the three-decker was strewn with skid-marked underwear, which Marl's mom dutifully whisked up.

That conversation was a frustration-and-verbal-masturbation cocktail.

Jus awoke back in the real world . . .

Jus and Marlene: The Sail Loft, Boston's North End

Jus certainly had reservations about letting his guard down. To his mind, dating at his age basically meant that you were cleaning up some other guy's mess.

"I actually never thought that you would call me," eyelash-batting Marlene quipped as Jus turned off his cellphone.

"My apologies, Marlene. I had to go down to Florida last minute on business. Duty calls, as I'm sure you can understand."

"Must be a big case."

"Not a slammer," replied Jus. "Kind of business as usual, but I guess in my world, business is never usual."

Marl was envious. "Shit. I need to go over to the dark side and set up shop on your side of the tracks as defense counsel. Life must be profoundly more interesting," Marl said, thinking out loud.

"Interesting indeed," shared Jus. "But sometimes interesting is not necessarily better or easier . . ."

Marlene nodded, smiling, and poked at her salad.

Jus gazed out the window and into the harbor for a few moments, and then said, "Hey, have you ever noticed that the same swans who yearn for you to throw them some bread crumbs are the same nasty birds who will hiss and bite your finger off five minutes later?"

Marlene responded with, "Of course. Life lesson number one."

As the sun began to set, so did Marlene's defense mechanisms, which were as solidly fortified as Dorchester Heights, once occupied by Henry Knox in 1776.

"You know, Jus. It's such a nice night. Would you like to maybe take a walk along the waterfront? It's so pretty just after dusk. Plus, my place is only a few steps away," Marlene said from the side of those rose-petal lips.

"Marl," Jus responded. "I am flattered and would love to go, but you seem quite conservative . . . and perhaps such risk-taking might not be characteristic?"

Marl thought for a moment. "The risk is all yours . . ."

"Check please!" demanded Jus.

Aboard the *Whitefish*: Ten Miles East of Thatcher's Island

The hurricane within Captain Caleb's head was spinning faster, as if traveling over warmer waters . . .

At his core, Caleb was a good man. Perhaps not a true mensch, but his flaws were few in the great scheme of a world where people had to compensate for their large inventory of sins.

He inadvertently inhaled a gnat while staring intently at his two separate GPS screens, and immediately he swallowed it in hopes that the invading insect might be a tsetse fly—anything that might generously put him to sleep and make this living nightmare go away.

While Caleb plotted their course, First Mate Sputnik was busily breaking out the first-aid kit to tend to the wounds of the fishing charter guests, who had spent most of trip thus far drinking beer, tangling lines, and slicing their fingers and wrists with rusty fishhooks, which, of course, sort of hurt as they pierced the skin but were brutally painful upon removal.

The natural anesthesia of a solid morning buzz-on would spare Sputnik the irritating sound of the incessant whining of a typical landlubber.

The guests who were not being Nightingaled by Sputnik were enjoying the consistency of the ten-minute intervals of dry-heaving over the side of the boat, courtesy of Caleb's uncanny ability to maneuver a vessel as to maximize the clutches of seasickness.

Sputnik yelled up to Caleb, "Hey, Cap—if these guys keep pukin' over the side like this, we won't need any more of that chum slick. What should I do?"

Caleb yelled back to the deck, "Have them pop a few more Bonines and make 'em switch over to light beer . . ."

Sputnik chuckled to himself as he recollected that famous

cockney-accented line from *Mutiny on the Bounty*: "'E just needs a lit'il sweet wawter to wush out 'is goots . . ."

Capt. Caleb was worried. And worried he should be.

Most of his fellow fisherman who were forced by economic necessity to resort to an operation like this would usually do so at 3:00 A.M. and roughly 100 miles northeast of the present location of the *Whitefish*, as to utilize the cover of darkness and distance to maximize the odds of a successful mission.

Caleb, however, embraced the opinion that such proceedings might actually be all the more likely to attract the attention of a patrolling Coast Guard cutter, versus trying to pull it off right under their noses in broad daylight, with a boatload of civilians.

As the waves tauntingly swashed by, Caleb could not help but the feel the weight of the guilt for what he was about to endeavor.

While he felt that he was jettisoning a slice of his soul, he also knew that he had profound responsibilities. After all, he was not just a proud captain, but he was no less proud of his roles as father to his daughter and husband to Leslie, even though he expected the FedEx truck to arrive any day with the divorce summons.

Caleb viewed himself as an old-school provider, and he would do whatever it took to ensure the safety and comfort of his family. At times, when that fog bank of self-pity would waft in from the east, he would quietly curse Leslie for knowing damn well what she had gotten herself into by marrying a man of the sea.

Her family quite openly disapproved of their Southern belle princess marrying some rogue, salty dog from Gloucester, but the joke was on them for Caleb was well known on the North Shore as one of *the* most handsome catches on the coast.

All he needed was a good scrubbing, a close shave, and a shopping spree at Nordstrom, and Caleb could have passed for a Newbury Street male model.

To be sure, Leslie was not some helpless waif clutching her nightgown every night, staring at the ocean while busily massaging rosary beads while awaiting the safe return of her dashing pirate.

More often, Caleb would be washing the boat when he received a text demanding: "Pick up Milk. I'm in the middle of a huge land-acquisition closing . . ." For whatever romance Leslie might have found in his profession years earlier had eventually weathered into something like pure contempt.

However, it was not always like that. There was a time when Caleb and Leslie were surely in love and acted like lovers.

Her abandonment of him was, at first, emotional. This was followed by the proverbial shunning of the physical connection—the ritual celebrated in the marriage bed. Caleb's self-esteem and sense of self-worth sank to the ocean floor like a barnacle-encrusted stone. His idea of being a man was cast into the air like a flock of clay pigeons . . .

Chapter 19

Caleb and Leslie

(While Courting)

"Leslie, you ready to go? Make sure you pack enough for an overnight."

"Caleb Frost. Where are we going? Am I being abducted?" asked the beautiful blond Leslie.

"Yes, in some sort of twisted way," replied Caleb. "But my guess is that you'll be treated quite well as a prisoner . . . and you might even develop some strange crush on your captor—you know, a little Stockholm Syndrome."

Caleb was excited to whisk Leslie away. He worked so hard and rarely had the time to get away for an impromptu overnight, but he was so crazy about Leslie that he was inspired to take a detour from his everyday life and engage in an adventure with the woman that he adored.

They loaded their bags, climbed into Caleb's pickup, and got on the highway, soon heading north on Route 95 and onward to a stretch dubbed the Maine Turnpike.

He promised her that it would not take too long. Caleb knew that Leslie, being prone to both car sickness and sheer boredom, was no fan of long road trips.

Caleb finally pulled off the highway and followed a side road for about fifteen minutes until they arrived at the quaint little town of Ogunquit, Maine. He drove down the main street until he found their night's lodging, the Anchorage Inn.

"Caleb. This is so cute. How did you find this place?" queried Leslie.

"It's actually been here for a while," the captain responded with the lightest of sarcasm.

Caleb parked the pickup and told Leslie that he would be right back, as he just needed to go into the office, settle up, and grab a key.

Minutes later, he carried their bags to their room, which was quite modest yet presented a panoramic view of the Gulf of Maine and, if one looked beyond, a deep blue oblivion.

Leslie was overwhelmed by the beauty of the setting and the imagination of her lover. He rarely showed much emotion, but obviously he had put a lot of thought into this getaway, all to make her happy.

And she wanted to reward him . . .

"Caleb," she purred. "Come here for a moment."

He approached her with a broad smile, and she kissed him deeply and passionately. She felt so happy and alive. Ogunquit certainly wasn't St. Barths or Palm Beach, but Leslie recognized that Caleb's thoughtfulness and effort illustrated how passionately he felt about her.

The two lovers proceeded to christen their temporary home and then lie together talking.

"Caleb," she said. "I know that at times you think that my family doesn't like you because you're a fisherman and they figured I'd be with some Harvard investment banker type. But that's foolish—I don't want that. They only value money, and their women are just trophies. Everything is a façade. With you, though . . ."

She touched his arm and entwined her fingers with his. "You're a man of the sea. Of nature. And you value what's important in life."

Caleb was quiet for a moment and then responded, "Yeah, I do feel inferior around your dad and your brothers. But I lead the life that I was called to. I couldn't bear to show up in a tie every morning at some bank and follow orders and prepare reports that never really showed anything or went anywhere. Or to have a meeting about the upcoming meeting, and then have the actual meeting, and then have a meeting to recap the meeting that we just had. To be concerned with who 'reports' to whom. How do you 'report' to anyone unless you're on the front lines in Afghanistan? What else is 'middle management' but people whose sole job is to justify their positions all day, while never really doing anything constructive at all?"

He paused and stroked her hair, then concluded, "No, I'd rather be a pissant fisherman and actually 'produce' something with my life."

To which Leslie gave him the deepest, most probing kiss that Caleb could have ever experienced . . .

Feelings of comfort and tenderness did not come easily for Captain Caleb Frost.

He remembered the first time that Leslie invited him to a family gathering at the prestigious Corinthian Yacht Club in Marblehead. The old Alabamans loved to sport a glow at the club. They enjoyed making their presence known by smashing the occasional whiskey bottle or requesting "Free Bird" from a bar mitzvah DJ.

It was very exclusive, and Caleb was worried that the club security was going to insist on a blood sample to ensure that it showed the proper shade of blue.

He remembered Leslie walking him into the grassy reception area, where all of the women were dressed as models, and the men sported the finest that Giblees had to offer this season. For his part, Caleb did his best with his cleanest blue jeans, a pair of shoes that did not smell like oily herring, and a blue blazer that he had picked up a few years earlier at Marshall's. He would have even donned a necktie if he had any idea as to how to affix one to his neck.

Leslie walked him over to meet her brothers and to introduce him to some of the other members who were attending the event.

"Caleb," said Leslie, "this is my brother Devon. Devon, meet Captain Caleb."

"Oh," replied Devon without moving his jaw. "My sister has mentioned your name many times. She's told us how you are quite the Gloucester fisherman . . ."

He paused for effect before adding, "However, I don't smell it at the moment. Perhaps some Old Spice has saved the day."

This little witticism was met by a chuckle from several other members standing nearby.

Caleb was not so amused. He saw where this was going.

"No, Devon," he replied calmly. "I'm actually a hundred-ton master captain, and we make our living perhaps a little differently than you may be aware of. But it's honest work, very much traditional."

To which Devon responded, "Well, I hope indeed that it's quite the living indeed, for as you can surely see, my younger sister is quite fond of the finer things in life. However, I am quite confident that you must have that all figured out quite nicely."

When Caleb said nothing, Devon continued, "I'm sure that when you were planning your future and envisioning a woman as fine as Leslie by your side, you must have sketched out your path to prosperity and how to ultimately make her comfortable—yes? Surely, that was in your plan?"

All Caleb wanted at the moment was the harpoon that was affixed to the bow of the *Whitefish*. But he set this thought aside, smiled politely, and responded, "Actually, Leslie and I always spend time together out on the sea, gazing with wonder at all of its gifts. We've never discussed the need to purchase a McMansion or to lease a Ferrari. Our early days, when we were just getting to know each other, were much more endearing."

Devon replied, "Mister—oh sorry, I mean *Captain* Caleb. You are quite poetic in your prose. I just hope such rhymes and verses will have the same effect on my sister when she realizes that she will never again reside on the soft, powdery sands that flirt with Mobile Bay."

Caleb swallowed a slug of wine and most of his pride. Leslie grabbed his arm and let him to the shrimp cocktail table.

"Caleb, I am so sorry," she said. "I know that my family can be overbearing, but it's not how I feel. You are a good man. A beautiful man, and ten times the man that any of them will ever be. I only want to be with you. Just you . . ."

She squeezed his hand and sighed. "I don't need eighteenth-green seats for the big golf tournament, nor do I need to fill divots after the last chukka. I only want to be in your arms and be honest and true. Just you and me. Just you and me . . ."

She saw Caleb relax and smile back at her, and then she continued, "I would jettison this fake world tomorrow if you would whisk me away from all this, take me on your boat when the seas are calm, and I hope the boat can accommodate three, because I want to have your baby and live happily ever after."

Caleb gave her a gentle yet meaningful kiss on her soft, pink lips, and he dreamed of ways he could fulfill her every wish.

He would persevere. He would make her happy. He vowed to make Leslie proud that she was his partner. No matter what it took. However far he had to push either himself or his ability to make the dream happen.

At that moment, there were no boundaries . . .

Back to the *Whitefish*

As the other vessel approached to the port side of the *Whitefish*, Caleb played into the *Whitefish's* VHF radio some haunting classical music, thus commencing the agreed-upon communication signal.

"Ever hear Bach's 'Bouree in C-Flat Minor'?" asked the approaching Canadian captain, citing a musical key that doesn't exist.

The Gloucesterman froze.

"N-No . . . ," he replied. "But I have heard that piece quite artfully adapted to F-flat major." (Another musical apparition.)

Sputnik, surreptitiously monitoring the exchange, turned to a particularly annoying, snotty guest. "Dr. Grimm. You familiar with something called 'Bach's Bouree'?"

To which Grimm immediately responded, "Ah, yes indeed, Mr. Sputnik. Such a beautiful sound, *bien sûr*. I was once invited by the British ambassador to Austria to witness its performance in a lovely park in Vienna on a most exquisite July evening."

Captain Caleb's thoughts quickly flashed Leslie's painfully beautiful visage, and he sought relief in the intoxicating salt air.

As the two vessels approached port side to port side, Sputnik caught a mooring line thrown by a Canadian deckhand who looked as though he was on his fourth day of a seawater cleansing diet.

Caleb yelled across to the Nova Scotian pilot, "Hey Cap! It seems we're a bit low on bait. Do you think you have any herring to spare, just until we get back to port? I'll gladly make you whole the next time you're in our waters. Just give me a hail on channel 12."

The Canadian fiddled with his two-way radio and then replied, "Yeah, I s'pose I could spare a bale. You're in luck too—the stuff is real fresh. Send one of your guys up to your bow. We'll throw it over . . ."

Without being told, Sputnik made his way to the front of the *Whitefish*. In less than a minute, the transaction was consummated. So easy . . .

The Canadian yelled over, "Cap, I'm gonna stay tied up to you for just a few more minutes. I'm hearing a clank in my starboard engine and I just want the guys to take a look before we shove off. No more than five minutes, okay?"

"No problem, take your time," replied the Gloucesterman. Frost knew perfectly well that there was no mechanical malfunction with the Canadian vessel, but its captain wasn't going to let Caleb out of his sight until he received confirmation that the money to fund this transaction had been wired and was in good order at the Bank of Canada in Halifax.

A few minutes later, the Canadian yelled over, "Looks like we're in good shape. Everything seems to be in order with the engine. Safe trip home, Captain . . ."

A few hours later, the *Whitefish* pulled into port. Caleb was beyond exhausted, but was very proud of how well Sputnik had served as a colleague on this mission.

As the guests and ancillary crew members began disembarking, Caleb realized that now he only needed to transport the large duffel bag from the boat to his truck. Countless times over the years everyone on the docks had seen Caleb and Sputnik unload gear after fishing charters, and this time nobody would be the wiser.

He told his first mate that he was going to make the delivery, and he'd be back in a couple of hours. Sputnik assured him that he could clean up the *Whitefish* and settle her down after the long voyage— maybe even cruise her across the harbor to take on diesel.

As Caleb walked up the gangway, he marveled at how easy this was—stressful, but easy. This caper would be the answer to all of his financial prayers. The fact that it would come at the expense of so many tortured souls certainly weighed on him, but he was actually pretty talented at relegating those thoughts to the farthest reaches of his mind.

As he approached his pickup truck, he took the keys out of his pocket and was about to insert one in the door lock when suddenly he heard a loud click and felt cold metal against the back of his head.

"Hey, Captain Crunch," someone said in a low voice. "Don't turn around. I think you have something that you're going to hand over friggin' pronto or I'm gonna splatter your feeble brains all across your Silverado. I ain't gonna ask twice, you pole smoker . . . I heard that you're quite popular with the Downtown Dykes."

Caleb felt the warm urine flow down his leg, and he froze in shock and disbelief. After all that time, effort, risk, and mental torture, he was being goddamned robbed.

"H-How did you know about my voyage?" he stammered. "And why would you do this? How could you?"

The thief merely responded, "Let's just say that you and I have some mutual friends, and loose lips sink the proverbial ships. Plus, you made it too damned easy. Now, fuckin' drop the bag. You got three seconds. One . . ."

To raise the count to two proved unnecessary, for Caleb gently tossed his financial dream to his right, toward the back of the truck.

"Now, get in the bed and lie face down," ordered the voice. "Count to 300. We're watching. If you're only up to 299 when you raise your head, my sniper friend will remove it. And he never misses . . ."

As Justin watched through the rifle scope from quite a distance away, he relished the idea that Darby would have at least a half-dozen ideas about how to wholesale this poison without getting their hands dirty.

It was ingenious on Darby's part. Talk Jester Chauncey into fronting the money for the buy. Captain Caleb does all the dirty work and procures the product, while taking on all the risk associated with the Coast Guard and navy patrols. Then, via Meyer and Jus, Darby steals the product in order to wholesale it (let some other knuckle-draggers actually move the shit on the street), while Darby, Jus, and Meyer get paid by the wholesaler and Jester is left holding his crank. Old-school brilliant . . .

The captain crawled into the back of his truck and lay face down like a disgraced animal. A cold, cruel breeze came out of the east, snuffing out the sound of the fleeing marauder's wheelchair as well as Caleb's dreams of financial freedom for himself and his only daughter.

Chapter 20

Jus and Marlene

The Perfect Storm *had nothing on Justin and Marlene*. The hurricane forces converged, and nothing short of historic was created.

The two perfect physical specimens shared with one another every ember that they could draw from their respective fires: passion, intensity, rage, pride, lust, and in some strange way, competitiveness.

Savages would have danced a softer ballet . . .

Jus was no stranger to the physical act, of course, but Marl was not quite so well acquainted. What bothered Jus was that this particular specimen presented a unique challenge. He was not merely attracted to her body and her primal scent. It was her mind that was clouding his.

His head was already a bit cloudy from partaking of the grape, but he remembered soft ripping. And every time that he ripped one of Marlene's inviting undergarments, his head swirled with the thought that this can't be real. Jus pondered the question as to whether or not it was the aftereffect of afternoon drinks, or maybe it was simply that he found her stellar. Like a moonbeam that danced over him.

With every rip, she gripped him harder, begging him not to stop. He gently placed her on the bed and kissed her stomach—although not necessarily to please her but instead, given Justin's characteristic selfishness, to "prepare" her for his inevitable entry.

Marlene, with a cat's sense of the environment around her, knew this, and yet it did not bother her in the slightest. In fact, it increased her arousal and anticipation.

She yearned for Jus. She desired to conquer Jus.

Little did she know that she was dealing with a man whose heart had turned to granite many years before.

As the two danced the age-old waltz, they deeply kissed, feeling the rain that was beginning to come out of the northeast. They avoided eye contact while focusing on the physical connection, which was indeed truly primal.

They finished together and found solace in their pillows as they parachuted down, exhausted.

Jus rolled over and climbed out of Marl's soft bed, then walked into the kitchen and pulled out two tumblers which he modestly filled with two fingers of Crown Royal, followed by two of Canada Dry and some half-melted ice.

Returning to the bed, he handed one glass to Marl, who accepted it like a baby bird being given a fresh worm.

"Thank you, dear. That was wonderful—an unexpected surprise," purred Marlene.

"What was unexpected? Jus replied. "Us leaving the bar to go roll around on the first date, or the fact that you let your guard down and actually smiled as we joined?"

"Fuck you," said Marl, propping herself up on her elbows. "How do you know anything about my guard?"

"Oh please," said Jus, sitting on the bed beside her. "You may as well present it like a drive-in movie from the seventies. You know, the kind where the foggy film is projected onto a torn tarp, and you hang that crackly old speaker on the inside of your car window—and the big victory of the night is either sneaking a handjob during an action scene, when all eyes are on the big screen, or sneaking in two of your buddies for free by locking them in the trunk."

"Must you always be so unabashedly charming?" queried Marl with a wry smile.

She quietly sipped her drink for a few moments and then said, "I'm thinking. As I lie here with you, naked as an egg, I can't help but wonder—how does this painfully good-looking professional guy come waltzing into my life and flash enough charisma to literally charm the pants off of me? Just so you know, flyboy, that is extremely rare!"

Justin arched his eyebrows, lightly mocking her.

"You are almost mythical," she went on, "like that folklore at the courthouse, maybe you've heard the story—there's this young, handsome Boston attorney who actually moonlights as a high-paid assassin. It's so silly—but it would make for a great beach novel."

Jus softly chuckled as he momentarily turned away with a subtle frown. Then he leaned over and gently caressed Marlene's soft hair while their tongues met in a passionate kiss.

While Jus was certainly no stranger to sex, a meaningful kiss was an incredible rare sensation for him—almost like a foreign language that he had never really learned to speak without difficulty.

Abruptly pulling away from her, he said, "Hey, Marl. I have a surprise for you . . ."

To which she responded, "I hate surprises. Just tell me what you have in mind."

"No, I can't do that," he said, reaching for his clothes. "Let's jump in my car. I love spur-of-the-moment road trips, and I want to show you somewhere."

Marl rolled her eyes and pretended to be annoyed, but in fact she was intrigued and more than a little flattered. Nobody had ever made her such an off-the-cuff proposal before.

Minutes later, the two jumped into Jus's Maserati and shot up Route 93 until they reached the junction of Route 128, and then proceeded northward, past Peabody and Danvers, until Jus pulled off the highway and headed east into the quaint New England town of Manchester-by-the-Sea.

Manchester was a perfect town for budding lovers—beautiful seaside vistas, plenty of North Shore charm, and yet few of the pesky tourists that flock to Marblehead.

Jus proceeded through town and pointed out the wondrous backdrop of the harbor and a few of the magnificent North Shore mansions.

Marlene stared in awe. This was certainly a far cry from where she grew up, and it amazed her that people actually lived this way, yet, as they passed one fine home after another, she was puzzled not to see anyone in the yard or in the driveway. She would be dancing on the front lawn if she lived in a place like this.

Jus finally parked the car beside a perfect beach. He got out of the car, popped the trunk, and withdrew an old-fashioned picnic basket.

"You see," he called out to Marlene. "I snuck some contraband for our trip right under your nose."

Marl responded, "Okay, Romeo—I'm impressed. Where are we?"

"Singing Beach," replied Jus. "And in a moment, you'll see why it's called that."

The two new lovers walked hand in hand over to the sand. There was a gentle southeast breeze that stroked their faces with a soft caress. The day was magnificent. The kind of day where two people in love truly believe that it was created only for them.

"Okay, take your shoes off and shuffle your feet," Jus instructed as Marl first stepped onto the beach.

She complied and then said with amazement, "Hey, the sand is squeaking . . ."

"No," said Jus. "It's 'singing.'"

Marlene beamed a smile and suddenly felt very warm and at peace. All her life, she had put so much effort into building up her walls and laying her bricks that it felt emancipating to let her guard down and let her romantic companion be her tour guide.

Off in the distance was the deepest blue she had ever seen. The cold North Atlantic can certainly rise up in fury, but at the moment it was soft and gentle, as if inviting the new couple to admire its beauty.

Jus picked a spot on the eastern side of the beach snugged up against a rock cropping. He had brought along a blanket which he laid down along with the picnic basket. Barefoot Marlene immediately sat and treated herself to slow, deep breaths of the southeasterly breeze. She found the salt air nothing short of intoxicating.

Jus's selection of that particular destination was by no means random. Back when he turned sixteen, Jus got his driver's' license and proceeded to cultivate a profound love for long drives up and down the North Shore. He would spend hours meandering on Routes 1A and 133, where he could admire the bucolic backdrop of the fields in Ipswich and the picturesque panorama of Essex.

One day he stumbled on the harborside town of Manchester-by-the-Sea and eventually ended up on the most beautiful beach he had ever seen.

He parked his car and began walking on the soft white sand, which answered his steps with an almost supernatural sound, so gentle that he felt compelled to remove his shoes and socks and just feel the cool powder beneath his feet.

He found a rock that looked like a perfect place to sit and for an hour just stared at the ocean, with the only sounds being the lapping of the waves at high tide and the cries of the seagulls.

It was only then, nearly two years after the traumatic curbside assassination, that Jus openly sobbed at the loss of his beloved Uncle Rick. The tears were uncontrollable, and he strained to breathe. His mind played a high-speed slide show of all of the memories and visions of his uncle, to the point where Jus was becoming dizzy and nauseous.

For years, he had often floated in visions of a recurring dream. It involved a fictitious event in which Jus was eight years old and found himself in an elevator with Uncle Rick and Meyer. As eight-year-old boys invariably do, the two started horsing around, and they proceeded to push and shove one another playfully against the sides of the elevator car. Uncle Rick gently scolded the boys and told them to knock it off. Ignoring Rick's protest, the boys continued to wrestle and shove, and Rick continued to tell them to cease their juvenile behavior.

At one point Jus shoved Meyer so hard against the elevator's back wall that the car suddenly stopped—it had obviously gotten knocked out of its track.

The boys were immediately frightened and became claustrophobic. Uncle Rick looked at them with a blank, glassy stare and then began to sweat profusely as he repeatedly pushed the alarm button. His face quickly turned to the color of alabaster.

Someone yelled from outside the elevator that they were stuck between floors and help was on the way.

Uncle Rick leaned against one of the elevator's side walls and slowly began to slide down the metal sides until his legs folded under him, like a kindergartner sitting Indian style.

Finally, some firefighters forced open the doors with the jaws of life and jumped in to retrieve Jus's uncle, who by now was obviously very ill.

The boys crawled out next, and Jus noticed that the firemen and EMTs laid Rick onto a bright blue carpet and began to administer CPR. But it was too late—Rick was already dead of cardiac arrest.

In the dream, Jus began screaming, "I'm so sorry! I'm so sorry! I should have listened and stopped. I didn't mean to kill you! I love you! I didn't mean to kill you!"

It was there that the dream ended every time . . .

From then on, once he had discovered it, Singing Beach would become Justin's personal sanctuary. Whenever life dealt Jus a particularly nasty curveball, he would immediately drive to Manchester. And he would, of course, always visit the beach after every hit assignment, not just to reflect and decompress, but also to prop up what little humanity he had left . . .

Jus opened the basket and began to lay out the provisions he had selected. He first handed Marlene a wine glass and then popped the cork from a bottle of Pinot Grigio.

As he poured, she suddenly felt like Cleopatra, for she had never been so spoiled.

He then pulled out a cutting board and prepared a tasty snack of dill cheese with crackers and apple slices, along with a delicious dressing and small pieces of Swiss chocolate. All of this was done with enough care and witty charisma to conjure up memories of the Emeril Lagasse show.

"Sweets for the sweet, and cheese for the cheesy," he teased her.

Marl had never experienced anything like this before. The last time she was romanced on a beach was that horrible experience in high school. Today was a world away different . . .

The two talked and fell further in love by the minute. They cuddled and enjoyed the view, the breeze, the wine, the snack, and especially one another.

In a quiet moment, she realized why she was falling in love with him. While there certainly was a high level of coldness and distance in his eyes, he still radiated beams of boyishness and a kindly emotional generosity that Marlene couldn't help but dive into.

"Jus," she murmured. "What do you think our lives will look like in twenty years?"

"Most likely the same," he replied, "yet we'll be older . . ."

With that she gave him a gentle rap on the forehead. "No, silly," she said. "I'm serious. You and I are in a business where we're just hamsters on a treadmill. Day in and day out, it's all about production and results. As a prosecutor, I'm expected to render justice. But I'm dealing with victims whose lives have been ruined, and I'm just there to ruin more. There's no end. There's nothing to create. No picture to hang on the wall when we're done."

"Yes, responded Jus. "I know that feeling regarding our business . . ."

Marlene couldn't know then that one day she would understand Justin's business with profound clarity.

A Few Days Later: Commercial Street, Boston

Despite the exhausting, cement-like weight of his shoes, Jus calmly and clomped up the steps of his North End condo.

Jus could easily have afforded a tonier address, but still, this was the perfect living arrangement for him, just the thing to say to any curious eyes looking in that "Yes, that handsome young man is doing quite well"—but not so well as to raise suspicions. Every aspect of Jus's avocation needed to be carefully considered and carefully hidden. The sharp edge of every angle needed to be filed down.

To admit to himself that he was completely and utterly exhausted would be tantamount to admitting that age was beginning to serve up the appetizers at his mind's first meal of the day.

Jus refused to concede any such thing. Just a few more jobs. . . Just a few more jobs. . .

Then, he chose to believe, things would finally be "normal" for him.

Jus threw one suitcase against the door, only to find it give way, sending the bag tumbling three feet across the foyer.

To find the door unlocked was not a surprise. If anything, he welcomed the sight of his dear friend and brother.

"Meyer!" he hollered. "Can't you spell d-e-a-d-b-o-l-t?"

Upon hearing Jus's words, Meyer spun around the corner in his wheelchair while transporting two bottles of Harpoon IPA. "How was your day at work, my friend?" he asked cheerfully.

To which Jus responded, "Just swell, June Cleaver. . . Actually, you don't look like June. You have bigger cans . . ."

Deep down Meyer was insanely grateful for having Jus home in one piece.

Their friendship could not be examined or described, for indeed it was fraternal in that Meyer was the overprotective big brother trying to guide Jus in a world that only lured him to "mischief."

"Jus," he said firmly. "Grab a shower and get yourself another beer. We need to talk. I've heard rumblings on the street that there could be a piece of subcontracting available on which we might want to place a bid. If executed properly to the satisfaction of the clients, it could mean some real options for us to consider, *finally* . . ."

Jus just stared right through Meyer's skull.

"Jus," Meyer persisted. "I want *in* on this. I want back *in* on life!" He wheeled himself up closer to Jus and said, in low, measured tones, "I used to be feared in Iraq. Now I'm a part-time self-pity story, at least to some, or perhaps a Tuesday 3:00 P.M. human-interest story on ESPN 6!"

He took a swig of beer and added with determination, "I *will* be your partner. This is *the* most intricate 'downtown urban development job' ever attempted. And only you and I can pull it off . . ."

When Justin said nothing to this, Meyer tried another tack. "I take it back, Jus. As you know better than me, there are many who could pull it off."

Seeing the Jus still wasn't arguing with him, Meyer added, "However, there are *no* two partners who could pull it off *and* walk away as if just turning around from taking a sip of stale water from some playground bubblah . . ."

Chapter 21

Trav and McGill:
At the Office of Shea & Rizzo Securities

"Hey, McGill," said Trav, with real concern in his voice. "You see that report that we're supposed to fill out for the Compliance Nazis? The one asking who we sold those BeamTech shares to and why we made the recommendation?"

McGill immediately responded, "Hey, Trav—just be honest this time and fill it in as if you actually give a shit. I don't like the feeling on this one. The sharks swimming in our little pond seem a little too large of a species for the likes of our two-bit firm."

Trav was trying to comprehend the need for concern, but the fact that he was a bean-bag from the neck up was not helping the situation.

McGill was no atom-splitter himself, but for some reason an innate notion kicked in on this one and he instinctively knew that, despite Nick Murray's insistence that it might never be true, the old novice investment adage that "this time it's different" might unfortunately apply now.

"Hey, McGill," said Trav. "I don't really remember any of that Series 7 bullshit we were supposed to learn, but weren't the initial price projections on BeamTech going out of the barn pegged somewhere around eight bucks a share? So how did I end up selling it to that old crow, the Choate widow in Wayland, for almost fourteen dollars?"

Seeing that McGill had no answer for him, Trav went on, "I mean, shit, I didn't care at the time, for all it meant then was that my commission went up and I'd be drinking imported beer instead of domestic at the Pats game that Sunday . . . but looking back, I have no friggin' idea why the trade went down like that. Didn't care . . ."

McGill was visibly concerned, which unnerved even an alabaster brain like Trav's. Even a mosquito has powerfully ingrained instincts not to get swatted . . .

Darby

Fear was a very foreign emotion for Darby. Everyone's human brain contains a blind spot or two. For some it's trying to learn a foreign language, and for others it might be learning to hit a baseball.

For Darby McBride, it was the concept of fear, which he understood about as well as to how to decipher the Mandarin version of the *Iliad*. Certainly Darb did not scare easily.

As Darby pressed the gas pedal on his 1988 Cadillac (yes, he actually took pride in residing in a time warp—to him, it was classy nostalgia) upon entering the Callahan Tunnel eastbound through the spiderweb of traffic known as Logan Airport, he felt his shoulders tightening a bit.

Darb was one of the few key players left over from the old days— "kings of the street corners" back then, who now mostly moved about while immersed in shadows, not unlike Mad Max driving through a barren desert or Yoda hunkered down in some celestial swamp.

He was modern enough to know how to evolve in the wake of the complete and profound upheaval of the Boston underworld.

To the rackets, Darby and all that came with his persona belonged in a museum.

Guys like him now found themselves traversing the underworld landscape not as part of a crew who took over Lombardo's in East Boston on Friday nights, but rather as independent consultants—he quietly chuckled that perhaps he should be requesting 1099 forms from his various contract "employers" for tax purposes so that he could open a SEP-IRA and quietly build up a steady retirement account.

Life was indeed now different. It had changed overnight with the demise of the Angiulo crime family and the implosion of the Patriarcas of Providence. Whitey Bulger's flight from justice and his subsequent capture was the final nail in the coffin of the organized Boston underworld.

Darby rarely laughed at something that he genuinely found amusing. However, he almost spit up his small intestine in glee when he read Howie Carr's recounting of Whitey Bulger getting caught shadowboxing with his prick while in solitary confinement in prison. Darb had certainly done business with said celebrity gangster since Bulger first returned from Alcatraz, but he always felt filthy after shaking Bulger's or Stevie Flemmi's hand.

To Darby, the only legend from that illustrious generation to have any real brains or class was Johnny Martorano, as evidenced by where each of the three presently resided. Instead of serving hard time, Johnny was now busy asking his friends and neighbors how they like their steaks cooked as he stood at his yuppie built-in industrial gas grill on the porch at his suburban townhouse.

Hats off to Johnny, thought Darby McBride. He was really embracing suburban life. From what Darb heard, Johnny was contemplating going green and installing a solar-powered grill for next summer's entertaining.

The morning before, Darby had received the call that he was to meet Don Cistulli at Logan Airport and to act upon his instructions as to a final destination. It seemed that the don was "requesting" (demanding, of course) a personal meeting with Darby regarding some recent "developments" within the Boston underworld, or what was left of it.

This type of command performance was unprecedented, as it was well known that Don Cistulli very rarely left Long Island's Gold Coast and the insulation of his "retirement" after refusing to testify to anything other than running an illegal card game during his sixty-year career in the crime world.

Everywhere the don went, the FBI followed (and, of course, tipped off the press), and thus Cistulli's movements were never surreptitious, nor without well-documented footprints.

Despite his arriving by private Learjet with a back-door exit to the runway, the Boston media would be there to snap pictures and garner footage for six o'clock.

Darb was slated to meet the old don at a cavernous warehouse at the farthest end of the airport, which had once served as the cargo terminal for Butler Airlines. Darb reminisced about how much grass they had moved through that building over the years. It irked him that nowadays every clown who had overdue bills and a weak conscience was running heroin via commercial maritime and aviation transportation. To Darb, that type of move was low-rent. *Just buy a damn drone and strap a brick of "brown" to it*, he grumbled to himself. *Godless idiots with their stupid business practices and stupid choice of product.*

Darb pulled into the terminal parking lot, where an attendant ushered him around back. It was eerie in that there was nobody else around—nobody with a microphone or a camera crew. He had never seen any section of Logan so quiet . . .

Darb waited for ten minutes until a small yet elegant private jet taxied within 100 yards of his Caddy. The door's hydraulics slowly lowered the stairs, and immediately there appeared three impeccably dressed, dark-haired goons whose eyes roved like lighthouse beacons.

Next came the vision of a small, frail man who appeared to be in his early eighties and rather unsteady on his feet. He, of course, vehemently refused the assistance of the other men on the scene and slowly descended the metal steps.

This was not the arrival of the pope, and Don Cistulli was not about to kiss the tarmac of this godforsaken city—full of Irish rogues and assorted revolutionaries all the way back to the founding of the nation. The don considered America a wonderful land of opportunity, but his Italian ancestors had not exactly been welcomed upon her shores. Plus, "they" had wrongfully knocked off Sacco and Vanzetti, and that thought alone had the don ready to spit on the cement.

Indeed, Don Cistulli had a particular disdain for the Irish, for they were incapable of speaking without a thick tongue, or even enjoying an evening without being guided by a wandering prick. *Animals*, thought the don. It disgusted him utterly that the Irish and the Italians shared the same love for the Mother Mary—clearly, they had vastly different interpretations of her message, or so he believed.

Darby slowly opened his door, and in a very humble and respectful way he approached the don.

Cistulli smiled and shook Darby's hand. The don's smile could melt the hearts of the coldest of adversaries, immediately relaxing them, putting them off their guard, and gaining their trust.

Darby slowly offered a bow and kissed the old gangster's hand.

"Don Cistulli," he began. "It is with great honor that I welcome you to Boston. You look hearty and well. Your visit was a bit of a surprise, but as you know you have my unwavering respect and I will do everything that I can to make your visit a comfortable one."

With all the skill of an Indian snake charmer, Cistulli returned Darby's admiration: "Mr. McBride. You have my great appreciation that you have welcomed me on such short notice. Surely you know that such an imposition on my part is not without pressing significance. I wish you join me and my driver on our way to our final destination so that I may brief you as to the reason for my sudden visit. Please give your keys to Dante, and he will follow us in your car."

To which Darby presented the keys to the don's glorified coat-holder, and he gestured that he would follow Cistulli to the overly stretched limo awaiting the don. It was the only vehicle at the airport that day that was more anachronistic than Darby McBride's old Cadillac.

As the limousine pulled out of Logan Airport and onto Route 1A North, Darby knew not to ask where they were going. That would have been futile, and a profound insult besides.

He did notice that his Cadillac was riding in their wake through the heavy traffic, so Darb silently hoped that it was an indication that they would eventually leave him with the ability to drive away.

The don was quiet for the first few minutes of the ride, softly speaking a few words in Italian to his driver. Darby felt shame that after all these years he never learned the language of these people who were always, it seemed, either his beloved partners or his wretched adversaries.

Cistulli appeared rather tired, but pleasant. Only longtime players like Darby would know the real history of Don Cistulli, whose ruthlessness was the stuff of underworld legend, the scariest part being that the lore was neither fiction nor embellishment.

After several minutes of near silence, Cistulli turned slowly toward Darby, cleared his throat, and said, "You see, Darby, I wanted very much to visit with you for several reasons, not the least of which is that I was looking forward to discussing old times with someone who was there and had a working knowledge. As I age, I find myself becoming a bit of a victim of yearning for nostalgia."

Darby nodded respectfully.

"But before we wax poetic about days of yore," the don went on, "I have a little unfinished business that I need to discuss with you. A rather unfortunate piece of business, I fear."

Darby stiffened slightly at the word *unfortunate*.

"You see," Cistulli continued, "one night, some time ago, a certain niece of mine met quite an untimely and ugly demise on a boat in Boston Harbor." He shook his head sadly, then added, "Knowing her, she was certainly up to mischief, for she had a penchant for picking the wrong shell to be lifted."

Darby understood and nodded.

"At any rate," said the don, "she was shanty Irish . . . certainly not the sort of rogues with whom I could normally claim to be related. However, my brother was a horse of different color."

Darby just stared blankly yet respectfully at the aging mob boss and swallowed his pride in the face of the obvious racial insult.

"At any rate, Darby," Cistulli went on, "it was brought to my attention that the hit was the handiwork of a certain punk assassin with whom you may have an acquaintance. A lawyer named Justin McGee."

"Don Cistulli," replied Darby, "with all due respect, how could you know that it was McGee? Even I knew nothing of this . . . terrible, murderous mistake." Darby could feel his heart beginning to pound.

"You see, Darby," said the old don wearily, "when you get to be my age and have so much mileage on what you might call the influence odometer, information just seems to arrive at the door."

He paused, shaking his head, then added with a savage growl, "So let's just say that I fucking know!"

Darby was indeed frightened, and he understood immediately that this was very bad news for Justin. He was going to have to warn him, but do it in such a way that the don would never find out, lest Darby receive the same fate that awaited the young assassin.

His voice returning to a soft, dignified register, Cistulli continued, "So Darby, what I am asking, or rather ordering you to do is find this Justin McGee and bring just his trigger hand to me. The rest of him you can dump in the harbor, preferably near the scene of the crime. His ending up in a watery grave is what needs to be done, for it is now my duty to look after my brother's remaining quasi-wives' children and to seek justice and proper retribution when required."

Cistulli's face tightened for a moment, his eyes blazing with the old fire, before he relaxed, sighing and again shaking his head sadly. "Enough on that for now," he said with a shrug, "but please begin a thorough search. My intuition tells me that you may be able to find him in a timely manner, which is why I selected you for this assignment. Plus, the word on the street is that you have become a tad disenchanted with semi-retirement and that you're seeking a bit more activity. Yes?"

Darby smiled compliantly.

"I hate the thought of someone so seasoned and with so much talent and experience to be sitting on his hands, while the mind begins to atrophy," concluded the don. "I'll give you a week, and then we may need to have a little 'pep talk' just to make sure that your heart is truly committed to fulfilling my wishes."

With intense trepidation, Darby quickly sized up the overall situation. He found himself wrestling with the rare emotion of pure panic as he thought of the bodyguards in their little caravan—they were surely carrying automatic pistols or worse. Darby could only speculate that these entry-level henchmen assigned to protect the don probably thought that they were guarding some kind of aging, soft-witted Kris Kringle. They would never know the real don, for Darby doubted that Cistulli still possessed the same brain chemistry that boiled with fury like it did thirty years earlier.

If Darb had a sawbuck for every historical tale of the Don's malice, then maybe he could actually have the kind retirement that he so dreamed for himself. He recalled one particular yarn, a story from back in the late sixties, early seventies.

Boston's kettle was boiling over with mob activity, namely the internal warfare among Irish gangs that typhoon-poured blood over the streets of places like Charlestown, Somerville, and, of course, South Boston. It was these times that spawned the beginning of legends like Whitely Bulger, Stevie Flemmi, Frank Salemme, and John Martorano.

The way the story went was that Don Cistulli was then "on assignment" for the five families in New York to serve as a "presence" among the soulless, animalistic zombies who controlled the Boston underworld. For Boston is truly the American city of the Irish, only to be rivaled by that island nemesis, some 300 miles to the southwest, that was once dubbed New Amsterdam.

Of course, at the local level the Angiulos called the shots, but NYC felt strongly that a second set of Italian eyes was needed to keep watch on that cesspool to the northeast.

One of the don's requests when being assigned to Boston was that he be allowed to settle his family on the North Shore and not the South. "I want neighbors whose last names *end* with the letter 'O,' not *begin* with it," Cistulli would always quip when asked about his Boston outskirt of choice.

As a result, Don Cistulli relocated his young family to the quiet oceanside (and mob-ridden) town of Nahant, which had a substantial Italian American community.

Cistulli bought a rather unassuming home in order to avoid garnering too much attention, but he did have a commanding view to the northeast over the open and vast Atlantic Ocean. The don often fantasized that he could throw a canoe into the water and paddle to Nova Scotia if his little compound was ever raided.

He brought along his painfully attractive wife Belli, who was to be the source of numerous other Don Cistulli fury anecdotes over the years, and two young children, Constance and Anthony.

After the move was completed, the don immediately took to heading into Boston each morning and proceeding to the Angiulo headquarters on Prince Street, where he would commence the day's business activities.

Belli was, of course, in charge of the house and the children, which was a task that she embraced wholeheartedly. She was very old-world Italian and had an unabashed love for her offspring.

Anthony was enrolled at a private Catholic grammar school a few miles away, and he actually connected quite quickly with the other students, many of whom were of Italian descent. Anthony possessed plenty of passed-down charisma.

Constance was enrolled as a freshman at Our Lady of Perpetual Suffering Roman Catholic High School in Lynn, where, even though she was rather timid and shy at first, like her brother she was quickly welcomed by her peers. She heard whispers about her classmates' dads all being intrigued by her father.

This confused her very much, for while the don was certainly a doting father, especially with his daughter, he was a man of few words or overt actions.

However, Don Cistulli did indeed make his presence known around town rather quickly after Constance ran into a bit of an "issue" at Our Lady . . .

Chapter 22

The Tutor

It was Constance Cistulli who made the first mistake. It was not at all her fault, for she was a trusting, simple, and beautiful young student. Lacking the ambition to take on the world, she just wanted to make her dad proud. The don, for his part, loved nothing more than to play some soft music on the stereo and then marvel as she danced across the lawn with only the downy white sheets of perfect sails across the Atlantic horizon as her backdrop. To underestimate the connection between the Don and Constance would be to trivialize the bond between the moon and the tides. Simply put, she was enamored of the don, and the feeling was quite mutual.

Constance didn't really need any extra help with her scholastics. She reveled in learning more and truly wanted to strive at the highest level. To that end, she booked her first after-school session on a lazy, sluggish Tuesday.

A low pressure front sat stubbornly offshore like an unwanted visiting relative who decided to lease the couch and bring along both gray weather and a grayer disposition. Tad Bestori opened the side door to Our Lady, already late for his next tutoring session. The gig had been great for a few extra bucks, but certainly wouldn't provide him with a new Porsche.

Beginning that afternoon, Tad tried very hard to assist Constance with her studies, but he was unable to squelch a stubborn inborn voice that led him to become a little too "friendly" with young Constance.

And that's where went Tad wrong.

Tad's previous teaching job was in Woonsocket, Rhode Island, where he had become known as the greatest gift to secondary school literature. Tad taught his classes with diligence and poise, while constantly trying to tame the beast within.

After the first year, he was already revered as one of the top teachers in the state, and his charisma and finesse with all of the school administrators made him all the more valuable.

If only they knew of his weaknesses and shortcomings . . .

Tad never maintained a thought that was born of malice, yet he could not overcome his sickness, which ended up infiltrating the minds and bodies of several healthy young people.

One could refer to him as a monster, and that moniker might be appropriate.

In the end, Tad was the kind of mental and emotional underachiever who felt the need to prey on the innocent in order to drive up his own stock price, at least in his own mind.

Fast-forward. Tad's "tutorials" with Constance ended abruptly one fine afternoon with her racing home to the arms of her loving yet potentially monstrous father. As Constance sobbed in her father's embrace, the don understood immediately what had happened. Cistulli was a man who thoroughly subscribed to the concept of *weregild*—the old Anglo-Saxon practice of exacting "man-price" when a wrong has been committed.

Back when he was a child growing up in Brooklyn, he was a rather frail lad who approached the world with a profound level of timidity. Cistulli's father "expired" when the boy was only eight years old, and the whispering reflected a state of semi-panic in the neighborhood. Apparently, the elder Cistulli, named Sal, had gotten into a jam with a local crew who punished bad business practices the old-fashioned way. All the younger Cistulli knew at the time was that his dad was a local pipe fitter who worked hard and spoke softly. In reality, the elder Cistulli was laboring on the side for the Genovese family as a "collector" whose job it was to collect debt payments from the easy clients. Customers who would neither make a fuss nor raise a fist. (More troublesome clients could expect a visit from an "enforcer.")

Now, Sal Cistulli wanted nothing more than to ensure his son's future by getting him out of the neighborhood and on to a better life. After making his usual collections, he would deliver to his employers about 90 percent of the actual take, while diverting the remaining 10 percent to a Folgers coffee can in the basement of the Cistulli household.

This went on for quite some time, eluded the attention of Genovese bean-counters until one day they realized that Sal was perpetually arriving a little "lighter" than anticipated. The fact that Sal's quiet skimming was undertaken solely to build up his son's college fund was not going to hold up in the street's version of criminal justice.

When Sal found out that he had been made and that the Genovese's accounting people had put two and two together, he did not panic.

Instead he went home and gently kissed his wife of fifteen years. Then Sal kissed his boy and wished him a much better life than any he could ever provide. He instructed the boy's mom to take the Folgers can and hide it in a nondescript corner of the attic, and never to think about it again until it was time to support their son's education.

Little did Sal realize was that this sweet, timid boy would eventually receive a very different kind of education than what his father envisioned for him.

Having kissed his wife and his son, Sal went into the kitchen and, very uncharacteristically, poured himself a large iced-tea glass of Chianti. As the boy and his mother walked in and silently looked on, Sal gulped down the glass of wine and proceeded to look like a seagull that had just swallowed the front page of the *Boston Globe* that had washed up on the beach.

He then got up and politely asked his family to leave the room.

The boy was scared, but really at his age it was just instinct telling him to be frightened. There was no rational reason for the fear.

Sal walked out onto the creaky porch, where he heard every board squeak its opinion of what he should do.

He descended the rickety stairs, and walked on the very small patch of grass.

He then pulled a revolver out of his jacket pocket and slowly held it to his sweat-beaded temple.

All the while, the boy and his mother watched through the dusty window. They watched with reverence. They did not try and stop him, for they knew that he sought peace and was making the ultimate sacrifice for his family.

Suddenly, without fanfare, Sal pulled the trigger and immediately lay on the ground in the same position that he would assume for the next slice of eternity.

His son just looked on in horror, and within seconds a dark stain of urine began to spread down the legs of his pants.

He then vomited twice into an old Easter basket that lay in the corner, perhaps to purge himself of the vision of what had just happened. Almost immediately, he tried to focus on his mother and how he must now play the role of the man in the family.

His mom draped herself over the arms of a stately chair and began to cry the tears that would feed rivers over the next few years.

It was then that the boy resigned himself to the fact that he would strive to never let himself be anyone's victim and always to fight to be the one holding the strings.

Bastori, LaCava, and the Don

Though few members of the don's inner circle realized it, the underworld figure soulfully embraced American literature.

The vintage record player at the don's Nahant home, which might be expected to play Mario Lanza and Frank Sinatra was usually emitting smooth American jazz from its one feeble speaker while the don, quietly reading in the corner with a small glass of soft Limoncello while basking in the ember-orange glow of the fireplace.

The don embraced American literature above all, for America was a nation born out of faith, desire, hope, and vicious violence—the last part of that four-leaf clover often ignored by the history tomes.

He adored tales by Mark Twain, whose adventures were seemingly ceaseless.

He marveled at F. Scott Fitzgerald, whose work posed the jarring question, "What the hell have we done?"

His mind raced at the words of J. Robert Oppenheimer, "I have become death, the destroyer of worlds . . ."

The don often gazed into the darkening blues of the northeast sky in the afternoon. Surveying the vast Atlantic Ocean, he would constantly marvel at its beauty and power, although, due to his own hubris, he resented the fact that some being even more powerful than himself enjoyed the opportunity to create it first. He always took eager note of the Nahant high tide as it selflessly give away eight feet of its precious height to the mean low water that promised to reciprocate six hours later. Often, while he would admire and was humbled by the majesty of the ocean, his thoughts would turn to the works of Edgar Allan Poe.

Eight feet. . . Eight feet. . .

He had an idea to take his mind off what was basically murder. He much preferred to think in terms of Old World virtues like sacrifice and justice.

Eight feet. Six hours.

A lot of poetry could be written in six hours . . .

Don Cistulli posed the question to LaCava, who had worked for the Don for many years and was his most trusted employee.

"Tony," he said. "How long does it take that mortar to dry? The kind that you've been using down at that Everett construction site?"

"I dunno, boss," replied the wary lieutenant. "Maybe four hours or so?"

To which the don responded, "Okay. Prepare a few buckets."

To LaCava's credit, he had good reason to feed his perplexity, yet he could see an idea spinning in the don's head and did not want to interrupt the movement of such a violent whirlpool.

Later

As LaCava dumped Tutor's jellyfish shape onto the rock floor, the don could not help but be disgusted by how pathetic said pathetic soul appeared. Gazing upon weakness was a profound emotional aphrodisiac for Cistulli, and as a result his pulse immediately quickened.

"Tutor. This is your moment. The moment feared by all men. To be exact, you do realize that it's your last moment.

"The last time the world will have to endure your annoying, whiney, whimpering voice.

"The last time you will ever look around and cannot help but feel self-pity as you gaze upon the power of the world and the people around you. The last time you need to feel shame. And pain. And guttural fear.

"Probably the toughest part will be the moment when you realize that all of the guile and stratagems that you naively thought that you possessed have all been stripped away. Do you know what stripped them away? Do you know why you are going to die a death that will be nothing short of a poetic? Raw power. That's the answer. That's the culprit that is about to set you free to be with your maker."

LaCava removed the thick ropes that bound the guest of honor, for what was the point? He wasn't going anywhere, and if he could, the next stop would be suicide anyway.

Yes, the castration had been excruciatingly painful, but fortunately for Tutor, shock seized him quickly and he felt basically nothing.

His body had already been rendered devoid of any feeling or primal electrical impulses.

LaCava proceeded to stand Tutor up and place him inside the cliff's hard-rock crevasse. All three men could not help noticing the stark fragrance left behind by the slackening afternoon tide as it reached its lowest ebb.

It would take roughly another six hours for Tutor's new home to become, as it did twice a day, underwater property. Tough location to obtain a solid homeowner's indemnity policy.

LaCava tossed Tutor into the hole like a sack of empty clam shells, and Tutor immediately collapsed. With neither a glimmer of hope nor a penis, this was shaping up to be a challenging day for the young former educator.

Without further delay, the business of laying the bricks commenced. LaCava never fancied himself a mason, but this wasn't exactly atom splitting.

The don said to Tutor, "Hey, you ever read Edgar Allen Poe?"

Line of bricks. Then the cold slap of mortar. Line of bricks. Slap of mortar. Quite methodical, and it put LaCava in need of an appropriate song—a tune he could whistle while he worked. But he wasn't a Disney kind of guy. Then he smiled as it came to him — *All in all, another brick in the wall . . .*

After several minutes, Tutor's stringy body was covered save for the neck up. He tried to scream, but the damp air and pounding waves below muffled all sound. Fortunately for LaCava, that day the Atlantic decided to bestow upon the coastal town of Nahant a steady westerly blow that would squelch Tutor's pathetic screams even if he fed them through a Marshall stack. The wind would carry his horrific cries only to the whales at Stellwagen Bank.

The don patiently and serenely watched as LaCava methodically carried out his orders—to seal up the crevasse entirely, brick by brick . . . except for one small, neat gap, right at the top.

This gap would cordially invite the Atlantic Ocean to this deathly dance six hours hence, thus completing Tutor's watery resting place.

LaCava truly appreciated the artistic aspect of his work, for it would have been much easier (yet much more perfectly dull) to just stick one of Tutor's veins with a syringe full of WD-40.

LaCava chuckled at that thought. At least the poor bastard would never have a clogged artery again . . .

Tutor raised his head and took in every sound. Plunk. Scrape. Plunk. Scrape . . .

So methodical. Brick. Mortar. Brick. Mortar. . . The consistency of the sound was so welcome to the ears that the construction of Tutor's maritime tomb became relaxing, in some twisted way. As he was slowly viewing the construction of his own execution, Tutor remained uncharacteristically quiet. Either he accepted his fate, or he was in complete and total shock regarding what was happening to him. *Maybe a bit of both*, LaCava thought to himself.

"Hey Tutor!" shouted the don. "You like lobster?"

"S-sure . . . whatever . . . ," feebly replied Tutor through the spider-web of drool that had gathered across his mouth.

To which the don replied, "That's good. 'Cause they're gonna fuckin' *love* you!"

LaCava greeted this witticism with schoolboy laughter.

These were the last sounds attached to his pathetic life. His soul would never hear its yearned-for symphony.

"For the love of God, Don Cistulli!" pleaded Tutor.

"Yes, Tutor . . .

"Yes, indeed. . . For the love of God . . ."

Not exactly original words, thought the don. He remembered where he had read them first, and smiled . . .

Chapter 23

Darby and Justin

Darby entered the small, unassuming Back Bay coffee shop, shaking the water off his overcoat. The pale sky had opened up as he walked from his car.

Justin was already sitting down with a cup of hazelnut and a granola bar.

Darby slowly took a seat without saying a word.

Justin spoke first. "So, old Darb. Why the sudden need for a meeting? I did note the tone in your voice. You sounded profoundly frightened—which is certainly not normal, and that in turn makes me frightened."

Darby gently rubbed the unshaven stubble on his cheek and chin. "I'll get right to the point, Jus," he said matter-of-factly. "Do you remember how pissed you were at me when I told you that Crasha Maloney, that whore you took out with Meyer, the one on the boat, was related to Don Cistulli?"

Jus just stared without expression.

"Well, Jus," Darby continued. "The don called me for a command performance meeting. *He* hasn't forgotten the hit, and somebody—*not me*, by the way—let him know that you pulled the trigger."

Seeing no reaction from Jus, Darby went on, "He then proceeded to not ask, but command me to take you out as retribution."

Justin leaned back in his chair while almost dropping his now lukewarm Hazelnut.

Darby fixed his eyes on Jus and lowered his voice. "Justin, the only reason that I called you here is to grant you the proverbial Lynyrd Skynyrd three steps of a head start to get away. As you know, the don would literally draw and quarter me if he knew I was giving you notice that I was on your tail. I'm only doing this because, even though my heart might be the size of a walnut, I do have some strange affinity and respect for you."

Justin returned Darby's gaze but showed no reaction.

"That being said," Darby sighed, "I don't want the don to think that I botched the assignment, because I'll end up in the weeds. So, Jus, unfortunately I *am* going to have to come after you. I'm sorry."

Jus could not believe what he was hearing. It was like a benevolent doctor telling him that he needed to amputate a leg.

Darb continued, "My advice to you, old friend, is to get the hell outta town and don't let me find you. I promise not to look for you for forty-eight hours. After that, please pray to whomever that I never find you. Enjoy your coffee and the rest of your life, which I hope for you is long."

And with that Darby stood and began walking toward the door. Justin hoped it would be the last time he ever saw the aging mobster . . .

Chapter 24

Darby and Jester

"Jester, you can see we have a real problem here," Darby McBride warned S&R's CEO. "We can't have you saying anything more to the damn prosecutors, the FBI, or anyone else who might try and complicate our lives. While they're not dragging you before the grand jury just yet, it's probably just a matter of days. You need to shut the fuck up and shut it the fuck up fast!"

"Darb, what am I supposed to do?" protested Chauncey. "I've got my back against the wall here. For obvious reasons—professionally, and moreover on a personal level—I can't trust my snatch of a wife who's got a mouth that's busy with everything but what I want her to do!"

Darby shook his head. "Jester, Mrs. Chauncey won't make her tennis lesson with her cabana-boy lover on Thursday if I want to silence her for good. I have sound reasons to just send her express-mail to her eternal reward this very afternoon . . ."

"No, no, Darb," pleaded Jester. "Just give me a few days to calm her down. Please don't hurt her. Yeah, she's a gold-digging miserable bitch on wheels, but she doesn't deserve to be killed."

Darby's major concern was that while Jester was being pounded by the Feds, he might serve up Darby's little heroin smuggling project as a bargaining chip, even though Jester would never see any benefit from the caper because the contraband had "mysteriously" been stolen. Darby smiled to himself, however, for he, of course, would still keep all of the profits of the stolen "brown," thanks to his young *protégé* and his crippled sidekick. Darby had put everything in motion right under naive Jester's nose.

Darby retorted, "Jester, most who get iced don't necessarily deserve it, but shit, they get in the way of plans that are for the benefit of the greater good. Look at it like we'll take her by eminent domain, that's all."

Chauncey entered that thought into his own calculations.

"Think about it, Jester," Darby continued. "Envision the situation like we're trying to build a tunnel from Plymouth to the Cape, and the bitch stubbornly refuses to sell her land. That's all. . . Shit—goddamn government does it all the time."

Chauncey found himself willing to concede this point.

Darby saw that Chauncey's resistance, feeble to begin with, was wilting. "Jester, you're an old friend and now a business partner, too. I don't want to upset you or get you in a jam, but we desperately need to slow down this runaway train, lest we're all going to be pressing license plates. And mark my words, Mr. CEO, I'll see to it that you're sharing a cell with Brockton's nearest and queerest . . ."

Chauncey shuddered. "Darb," he said, "I'm supposed to play golf with the DA guys tomorrow. It was a friendly invitation on their part, but I know that it masks what will basically be an unofficial interrogation. I can't back out now—it's way too obvious."

"Unacceptable," Darb replied. "You can't go. Tell 'em you're sick and you can't play. Shit, people get sick. The game sucks anyway. Waste of perfectly good real estate—although, unbeknownst to the brass at Salem Country Club, they got a coupla deadbeats about four feet under the eighth fairway . . ."

"Darb, I'm not sick!" exclaimed Chauncey. "I can't lie! I'm a terrible liar. They'll see right through me!"

"Au contraire, Jester. You are an exceptional liar—you have perfected the craft to the point where you could write the goddamned instruction manual. However, if you lack the confidence, maybe that's where I can help an old friend.

"I'm not going to put you through the ringer on this one. I'm here as a coach and mentor, and I aim to help and be of sound assistance. I recognize that you're not built for this high-stakes type of game."

Darby gave him a pitying look, while Chauncey sat immobilized, looking appropriately pitiful.

"So, okay," Darby went on, "let's think, Jester. How do we convince the feds with conviction that you're sick and cannot play, thus keeping you away from probing questions and peering eyes for a few more days? What would finally get it through their thick skulls that you're not full of shit and that you need to recuperate a bit from a bad illness?"

Darby stroked his chin mockingly. "Hey, Jester. On a side note, you could always drive a golf ball really far. Would you say that's the strong part of your game?"

Chauncey brightened slightly. "Yeah, Darb. I've won the 'best drive' competition at the club three times in the last four years. There are plaques on the wall in the clubhouse. I gotta admit, I'm a bit of a legend of sorts when coming off of the tee."

Darb continued this thought: "So, Jester, when you drive a ball, not that I have any interest, but I do recognize the fact that there are elements of physics behind it all. So let me ask you: which leg do you lean on and thus favor during a powerful drive from the tee?"

"Well," Jester replied, "for me it's always been my left . . ."

Then, suddenly—*BANG!!!*

Darby McBride had just fired a furnace-hot revolver slug into his old friend's thick left thigh, which left a burning hole the size of, well . . . the size of a golf ball . . .

Chauncey said nothing, but just opened his mouth as air was involuntarily forced in and out of his body as it quickly approached shock. His eyes sort of floated in his head and trained on nothing. All Darb could hear was quick, short breaths, and all he could smell was singed corduroy.

Darb looked at Jester calmly as the CEO slowly collapsed onto the ground.

"So Jes," he said, "the good news is that now you don't have to lie about missing your tee time."

Darby chuckled. "The bad news is that we have about ten minutes to get you to a hospital and concoct a story about how you were randomly mugged by a street vagrant, and you were subsequently shot while bravely resisting."

"Now here, let me wrap his handkerchief around your wound before you bleed out. It doesn't look so bad—I think I missed the bone. Shit, I just had my cousin reupholster the backseat . . ."

"Y-Y-You're—*ow!* You're a c-crazy sonofabitch, Darby . . ."

"No, Jester. If I were truly crazy, I'd have your whole family in my freezer . . ."

Jus, Meyer, and Marlene

Jus greeted the day like any other with calm confidence, and yet he had that anxious pecking at his forehead from the controlled anxiety that hailed in another day on the "job."

This was to be a day like no other, however. He texted Meyer and asked him one last time if he was ready for this particular assignment—for especially after this one, there would be no turning back from the "life."

Jus washed up, placed a cup of Earl Grey in the microwave and began to pack his so-called day bag.

Jus tended to daydream when he was nervous. While some people's daytime thoughts might explore the future with eyes wide open, Jus tended to stay involuntarily fixated on the past.

It was an extremely "hot and windy afternoon that set the trees in constant motion," as was written by Neil Peart when Jus was just a young boy. Jus's uncle grabbed him and invited one of his baseball friends for "Saturday morning breakfast."

"Breakfast" always entailed making the rounds to the various spots that needed to be visited around town.

First stop. Jimmy's Tavern at 10:00 A.M.

Jus loved how his uncle would set him up at the bar and let him invade the freshly made popcorn. King for a day in a local dive bar on a Saturday morning—how could life get any better? Uncle Rick would invariable have to duck into the proverbial "back room" while Jus would sit and gaze at the wide TV screen, which in those days meant showing the infancy stages of ESPN's *SportsCenter*.

Jus would wait for about thirty minutes, chomping corn while his uncle, for all Jus knew, was counting the quarters in the pinball machines.

Invariably, Jus's uncle would emerge from Jimmy's room with both hands in the midst of an overly dramatic firm handshake.

Jus loved Jimmy's in-ground pool as well. When Jus was young, his uncle would let him visit and swim at Jimmy's pool as a reward for good grades, or sometimes for a solid swing of the bat during a little league game.

Jus would later learn that Jimmy was found face down in said pool with two in the hat, while the filter was running perfectly.

Every drop of tepid water cleansed to perfection . . .

Back to the Matter at Hand . . .

The high-powered rifle was easy to dismantle and reassemble, which made it especially handy on assignments that required a low profile, and the smallest possible briefcase.

How things had gotten to this point, Jus had no idea. It was inconceivable that the one time, literally the one time, he may have opened up his heart and betrayed his brain was being thwarted by his pitch-black occupation.

To most, this particular assignment would be insane, unimaginable. But Jus was not like "most," and anyhow it was to be very lucrative—in fact, a bit of a command performance. Those who wanted it completed and completed right insisted that Jus be the triggerman. They insisted to the point of making very concrete threats against the very person Jus loved most in this world (if he was capable of love at all). Meyer.

And clearly, he had to find a way to not harm the woman he loved—wow, that concept really jarred his thought process, and moreover he had to figure out how, simultaneously, to conceal from Darby the fact that he had scuttled the hit on purpose. If Darby knew, that would inevitably and immediately sound the death knell not only for Jus, but also for Meyer and eventually Marlene as well. It had to look like an accident.

In the midst of these considerations, Justin received a text from Darby that read: "Jus, we need to talk immediately. I met with Don Cistulli and he is especially upset about this nonsense that occurred in Boston Harbor aboard the *Annabelle Lee*. I am instructed to 'bring' you to him."

Jus ignored the message for now, for he knew what Darby was referring to, and this wasn't good. Darby was hired to hunt Jus down.

This was a high-stakes hand, and Jus uncharacteristically did not have the deck already stacked.

Jus would always shave before a job, for a sense of quiet, proud professionalism was key to the calm nerves that the sniper's profession required.

He zipped up his maroon briefcase and headed out the door to his car. His phone buzzed with a text from Meyer, serving as a stark reminder that he was ready and that there was no turning back.

Jus quietly and methodically set up the mini-tripod on the roof of the hotel, which overlooked the entrance to the Joseph Moakley Courthouse.

He noted the bitter irony of the fact that the most beautiful piece of real estate on Boston Harbor was reserved for felons, federal-law-breaking deviants, and government-payroll hacks. A courthouse could have functioned just fine in a neighborhood like Roxbury or Dorchester that could use the economic influx of money and pedestrian traffic, thus allowing for the utilization of the waterfront land by a high-taxpaying private entity. This really confused Jus, but at this particular moment such thoughts were low on the totem pole of his priorities.

With a soft cloth that was originally intended to remove finger-prints from iPad screens, he cleaned his weapon's military-like preci-sion rifle scope and prepared to seek out his target.

As Darby had discovered, Marlene's hearing was scheduled to break for lunch at precisely 12:15, and she should be exiting the courthouse in time to rendezvous with her girlfriend for lunch at 12:20.

Jus mounted the rifle on the tripod, checked the weapon's chamber, made sure that he had left nothing on the ground, and prepared to do what all assassins do best—patiently wait.

Periodically, he would use his small set of binoculars to scan the courthouse entrance and reception area for any unforeseen obstacles, such as extra police details or anyone resembling the FBI.

According to Darb, today was to be ostensibly a quiet day at the mammoth facility—business as usual, if there ever existed such a thing.

As he peered into the scope, Marl's stunning figure suddenly ap-peared in the main doorway. She looked profoundly out of place with her chiseled body and striking features, in stark contrast with the appearance of some disheveled underworld wise guy or overweight court officer.

If only Marl could see him. He envisioned her feeling his stare. She would look up, smile as if to say, "I'll be home soon, honey. Let me just get through this day."

According to Darby, Marlene Dunn was not going to just miss the rest of this day, but also would forego any others that she may have anticipated from this day forward. Jus had other ideas, though, and was still thinking of how to extricate himself from this real-life Scylla and Charybdis.

Another text notified Jus that Meyer was watching for any signs of trouble, and was thus far seemingly unnoticed by anyone in the area. His disguise as a homeless wheelchair cripple was only garnering sympathetic or scornful stares rather than suspicion.

Jus gazed through his binoculars and saw Meyer slowly snaking through the bustling entry area and stopping at every trash receptacle and unoccupied break table in order to stuff empty cans into the plastic bag that was tied to the back of his chair. For this assignment, obviously, Meyer could not use the Olympic-caliber chair with which he trained, but rather an old beat-up junker he had found at a yard sale.

Suddenly Marlene sat herself at one of the tables and began to tap on her phone, evidently to compose an e-mail or text message. This was not good news for Justin (or Marlene, for that matter), for Jus would have less of an excuse as to why he had missed his target, as this particular one was no longer moving.

Suddenly, Justin heard the rolling sound of thunder being delivered loud and clear by the pesky west wind. A storm was approaching, but still far off and nothing compared to the maelstrom that he was about to spark.

Jus was uncertain about his next move. This was not the movies where he could just try and take a shot only to wound, for all of the weapons in his collection were carefully crafted for one task—to kill with one shot. And Darby was well aware of that fact.

Jus's mind began to wander.

He thought back to the first time he ever saw Marl and how profoundly awestruck he had been.

Suddenly, a school minivan pulled up to the curb and let out what appeared to be a group of middle-school children most likely at the courthouse for a field trip or a mock-trial exercise. Jus noticed that one of the boys in the group looked shockingly like himself when he was that age. So full of wonder.

So full of excitement, dreams, and passions.

So full of . . . himself . . .

With that thought, Jus's blood turned to ice and his heart turned to stone. He trained his crosshairs on unsuspecting Marlene.

And squeezed the trigger.

Time stopped for Jus. Normally, within five seconds of a strike he was already zipping his briefcase and turning around to begin his escape from the scene.

This time however, he merely stared and listened. In his mind, he saw Fourth of July fireworks and heard the "ooh's" and "ahh's" of happy children.

The reality of the scene was quite different.

The half-dozen school kids who had just arrived glared in sheer horror, and every second that went by was greeted by another student's shriek of primal terror.

Jus couldn't bear to look at where the bullet had entered Marlene, but it looked every bit like a customarily accurate Justin McGee kill-shot.

The table and back wall next to where she was situated looked like a modern art student's first experiment with the color maroon, with the class being taught by Jackson Pollock.

Jus stood and calmly dropped his weapon and other equipment to the ground. He turned and slowly began to walk away empty-handed.

Surely the tools of his handiwork would soon be discovered: fingerprints, DNA, and all. A relentless hunt for Jus by every law enforcement resource in the Northeast would begin immediately.

Jus didn't care. He merely wanted a shower. Alone.

He thought to himself that maybe he would listen to Howard Stern on the way home on his Sirius radio in order to find a little chuckle, if there was one to be found.

Several people ran to Marlene's lifeless body. Two court officers gently picked her up and swiftly brought her into the courthouse.

This turn of events was certainly going to result in a nationwide manhunt, and Jus knew that he would have to go on the lam.

Perhaps the Georgia barrier islands, he thought to himself. Surely not Florida or Mexico, which is painfully stereotypical and trite.

An ambulance appeared in front of the courthouse within seconds, and two EMTs scrambled through the crowd that had quickly gathered. They rushed to where Marlene lay lifeless in the hands of the court officers who were tending to her. The first EMT to reach her feverishly sought a pulse, and frowned to his partner and said, "What kind of monster would do this?"

Meanwhile, thoughts were surging through Justin's head as he rushed to make his escape from amidst the madness of the scene. *At least I saved Meyer's life*, he rationalized to himself.

He of course knew that he was not fooling himself and that he had just committed the ultimate abomination—not only taking the life of his lover, but also breaking his own code.

She did not deserve it . . .

Chapter 25

One Year Later: Jekyll Island, Georgia

As Justin finished shaving and getting dressed, he reflected on he past year's events and felt a sense of awe.

He had so far eluded both the police and anyone resembling the likes of Darby McBride.

By keeping a relatively low profile and assuming a pseudonym, he so far kept himself off everyone's radar, except of course that of his new partners.

He still had both dreams and nightmares of Marlene and how wonderful, and yet tragic his times with her had been.

Over the past year, fortunately, he had not had to take a life and now considered himself basically "retired" from his horrid former vocation.

He wondered what his partners back at the law firm thought during those first few days after the hit as Jus literally disappeared, and he was desperately curious as to whether or not they had put two and two together and noticed how his sudden exit coincided with the last day on earth for a certain beautiful assistant district attorney. Of course, eventually the evidence Jus had left behind was discovered, and there was a nationwide manhunt.

His partners were stunned . . .

He could still smell Marlene's perfume. Taste her lips. Taste her perfect feminine sweetness . . .

And in some strange way, he actually felt her presence.

He enjoyed living on the boat at the marina. The club wasn't super-fancy, but the people were friendly and the food was superb.

He grabbed his wallet and zipped up the fifty-foot Cabo sport-fishing yacht to which he had treated himself several months earlier, a vessel that had proven itself to be so very handy for his occupation over the last year.

As he walked up the dock to the tiny marina restaurant, he remarked how wonderful the gentle breeze felt on his just-shaven face, and how wonderful the first apple martini would taste.

Justin asked for his usual single-diner corner table.

To which the hostess replied, "Ah, Mr. Baxter. Tonight, I actually need to get you a table for two . . ."

He was quickly greeted with "Hello, Justin. Or is it Tom Baxter? How Boston original."

That siren-like voice—he was stunned. The only thing holding his entrails in at that moment was a thick epidermis-&-bone cocktail. Justin's usually stone-cold heart raced like never before in his life.

"My guess is that you didn't anticipate having a dinner date tonight—yes?"

Justin just stared. With the sharpness of his former days, looking through a rifle scope . . .

Marlene appeared nothing short of an apparition, for her beauty was still so profound, even though one year ago Justin had attempted to assassinate her and silence that swan's voice forever. Close those eyes permanently.

And he had apparently failed . . .

"Y-You look s-stunning, Marl . . . ," stuttered Jus—the first time in his selfish life, in fact, that Jus had ever stuttered at all.

To which Marl replied, with a bit of a slur due to the speech impediment that had resulted from the head wounds received from her dinner companion twelve months earlier.

"Well, Jus . . . or should I call you Tom? No thanks to you . . ."

Justin just stared at what had to be a ghost, but the rational part of his brain knew that this was no apparition.

Marl just looked back at him with a wry smile, and then remarked, "Hey Jus, you seem to have spilled something on your shirt . . ."

Jus looked down, expecting, say, a ketchup stain on his $300 linen button-down, and subsequently he found it.

Only it was bright red and perfectly circular. Actually, it was a very pronounced scarlet dot, and it jiggled a little from side to side when he moved . . .

And said stain was trained precisely on his sternum.

Marl's wide smile was a combination of the Cheshire Cat and Medusa . . .

The End (For Now . . .)